PRAISE
KATIE MacALISTER

Memoirs of a Dragon Hunter
"Bursting with the author's trademark zany humor and spicy romance . . . this quick tale will delight paranormal romance fans."—*Publishers Weekly*

Sparks Fly
"Balanced by a well-organized plot and MacAlister's trademark humor."—*Publishers Weekly*

It's All Greek to Me
"A fun and sexy read."—The Season for Romance
"A wonderful lighthearted romantic romp as a kick-butt American Amazon and a hunky Greek find love. Filled with humor, fans will laugh with the zaniness of Harry meets Yacky."—*Midwest Book Review*

Much Ado About Vampires
"A humorous take on the dark and demonic."—*USA Today*
"Once again this author has done a wonderful job. I was sucked into the world of Dark Ones right from the start and was taken on a fantastic ride. This book is full of witty dialogue and great romance, making it one that should not be missed."—Fresh Fiction

The Unbearable Lightness of Dragons
"Had me laughing out loud. . . . This book is full of humor and romance, keeping the reader entertained all the way through . . . a wondrous story full of magic. . . . I cannot wait to see what happens next in the lives of the dragons."—Fresh Fiction

Also By Katie MacAlister

DRAGON REVISITED

An Otherworld Adventure

Katie MacAlister

FAT CAT BOOKS

CONTENTS

BECOMING EFFRIJIM

WHAT IS THIS?

This short story takes a deep dive into Jim's past, the reason he became a demon, and the meeting with Aisling...from his point of view.

If you're confused about who Jim is, what a Guardian does, and how a dragon can be a sexy man named Drake, you might want to dip into YOU SLAY ME, the book that started all the dragon shenanigans.

If you're a fan of Easter eggs, get ready to rock and roll!

DAY 1
Saint George's Day

"Yo, Garters, how they hangin'?"

The woman, who was bent over a raised flower bed full of lavender, sighed heavily before straightening up to turn and face me. "Ah, it's you. Effriflem."

"Effrijim, although I'm thinking of dropping the Effri part." I struck a pose that I hoped would sway her, even though I had little hope of doing so. In the six hundred years I'd been a sprite and Hildegarde was Sovereign, she'd yet to be impressed by me, although just a few years ago, one of the female sprites told me I looked like a dark-haired Norseman. I assume it was a compliment, since everyone knows how the Norsemen who used to pillage around here ended up winning over all the women, and not just because they bathed more than once a year. "Jim sounds good. Jim sounds solid. Thoughts?"

She slid me a look that would have felled a lesser sprite, and released another of her exaggerated sighs. "What is it you want, Effrijim?"

I took a step back when she added a bit of power to my name, making it sting. I thought about pointing out the head of the Court of Divine Blood wasn't supposed to hurt her employees, but decided I'd hold on to that bit of advice for a time when she wasn't looking so particularly cranky.

"I don't know. You called me. Also, you still miffed about Bingen?" I asked, sitting cross-legged on the grass, since she'd almost shot flames out of her eyes when I sidled toward the only wooden chair available.

She paused in the act of wiping the dirt off her hands. "What about Bingen?"

"The mortals," I prompted her, but when she just continued to stare at me with a face that could sour honey, I figured it was only right to clue her in. "The ones who filched the idea of the Court for some nebulous dogma they've been promoting. I mean, yeah, they are calling it Heaven and not the Court, but still, it's an obvious rip-off, and that sort of betrayal has to hurt, huh? I don't blame you for being crabby."

"Crabby!" She did a snorting thing that made me think of dragons breathing fire. "I am not crabby! I dislike the sea intensely, because shellfish unbalances my humors."

"I just don't get that," I said, shaking my head. "I, myself, love crab. I can eat buckets of it. That sweet, succulent meat dripping with melted butter … yum. But to each their own, right?"

"Crab," she said softly, her eyes narrowing on me. It was a pointed look, one that once again stung, and it was on the tip of my tongue to tell her she could absolutely hold her own in Abaddon if she ever wanted to become a demon lord, but the memory rushed back to me of a few centuries before when somehow, during a Court-wide banquet to celebrate the Sovereign's three hundredth anniversary, some deliciously magnificent crab ended up in what was an otherwise intolerably boring, bland fish soup.

Hildegarde had been stuck in the privy from midday until the following evening. Bowel Unblocking Day (as I'd referred to it, and the name kind of stuck) went down in Court history as a great mystery. No one owned up to slipping the delicious crab into the tasteless soup.

I smiled a big ole "ain't no crab on me" smile at the boss lady. The same sprite that thought I looked like a dashing Norseman also said I had a nice smile, but did Hildegarde notice? Not her. Truth be told, she was always complaining about me indulging in a few hijinks. Like there's anything to do at the Court if you don't get creative and stir things up a bit.

Hildegarde took a deep breath and pinned me back with another of those burn-you-at-the-stake eye-flame looks. "If I exude the barest hint of frustration and regret, it's because it is needful I must have a discussion with you. *Again*. And I find myself at the end of my limits with you, Effriflem. I've borne your pranks for as long as I could, given the debt the Court has to your mother, but as the centuries pass and your japes and pranks become more and more unbound, you leave me with few choices. It is for that reason that I wish to speak to you about an opportunity which I believe you may well enjoy."

"I'm all ears," I said, getting more comfortable on my spot, ignoring her complaining about my active sense of humor. It's not like I hadn't heard it hundreds of time before. "Well, not literally, because that would be weird having nothing but a pair of ears running around the Court helping people, but I was thinking that I'd like to try out some different forms. Dogs, for instance. Dogs are nice. Everyone likes dogs, right? I was thinking about a big leggy lurcher. Or maybe a greyhound. Or one of those black-and-white alaunts?"

"I don't believe—" the Sovereign started to say.

"How about a fancy spaniel? The kind with the curly hair? The ladies love those," I said, thinking about the local nobility's dogs.

"I really don't—"

"Of course, terriers are always fun," I added with a knowing wink. "Vermin hunts, am I right? Nothing but fun to be had there. Maybe a terrier is the way to go. One with a smirk. Hmm."

She breathed loudly through her nose a couple of times. "No terriers! No hunts! No dog form. Human form is right and proper for a sprite, and so long as you remain in the Court, you will adhere to my rules." She checked for a few seconds, then, with another narrow-eyed look flung my way, added, "Although that brings me back to the topic at hand."

"My human form?" I looked down at myself and made a face as I adjusted the leather codpiece that poked up from my tunic. "I got an upgrade when I made sprite third class, but I have to say it really hasn't been worth it. Now, a dog's form—"

"A vision has come to me, and that vision concerns a choice to be made," Hildegarde said hurriedly, averting her gaze from me. She dusted off the chair and sat, her hands clasped together, while her pale gold hair fluttered gently in the breeze. "Your choice."

"All right," I said slowly, feeling a bit rushed, but willing to take the plunge, nonetheless. "I'll go for a black-and-white alaunt. No, a spotted lurcher! Although they don't have much mass to them ... alaunt. I choose alaunt."

I swear she almost rolled her eyes. "The choice you need to make is which path you will take. One path remains here in the Court of Divine Blood, where you will continue to serve those immortal beings as need our help."

"I'd prefer to help mortals," I said, wriggling a little to combat the itch on my left shoulder blade. There was nothing behind me I could rub against, and the itch was too high to scratch it myself. Unless I was a dog. Then I would be able to scratch everything that itched. "Mortals are more fun. I like mortals."

"After the last time you were caught trying to convince mortals to rise up and smite their overlords in a blatant act of rebellion, your sphere of influence will remain within the Court and denizens of the Otherworld," she said with a tone that was so acid, it could probably etch glass. "As I said, you may remain here at the Court, fulfilling your duties as a sprite, or you may take a much more dangerous path, one filled with adventure and the unknown."

I sat up straight. "You what?"

A strained smile stretched her lips. Hildegarde didn't smile much, so it wasn't the friendliest look ever, but she was clearly doing her best. "I do not often encourage members of the Court to strike out on their own to discover their destinies, let alone the son of our most beloved former Sovereign, but due to my respect and honor for her memory, I will make an exception. Be warned, Effriflem! This is not a choice to make lightly—should you leave the Court to seek renown as you make your way, you will be entirely on your own."

I pursed my lips as I thought about it. I couldn't see much of a downside. For one, if I left the Court, I could adopt whatever form I wanted. Visions of a dashing, beefy hunting dog rose in my mind's eye, and I could almost feel the wind in my attractive fur as I ran through the forest, hunting things, eating whatever I wanted, helping mortals, letting them feed me fine meats and cheeses, traveling anywhere that took my fancy, discovering new foods … in other words, finding my own way rather than being tied down to a bunch of stuffy Court rules.

"It sounds good," I said slowly. "I like the part about renown. But I'd have to talk to Camio first."

"Who?"

"Camio. She's my friend. We've known each other since I was a wee little sprite, and she was a brand-new shiny demon sixth class. She's fourth class now, and has her eyes set on becoming a wrath demon, although frankly, I don't think she's mean enough for that. She also thinks I should switch to a dog form." I added the last bit just to drive home the point, but Hildegarde sucked in about half the air in the garden, rising as she did so with one finger jabbing at me.

"You are consorting with a demon?" Her voice, normally a bit screechy, lifted at least an octave until it hurt my ears. I quickly got to my feet and backed up a few steps, wary in case she decided to change me into something gross, like a slug. Or a newt. Or a wild boar.

"Not consorting," I said with my hands up to make sure they weren't turning into hooves or whatever sort of feet a newt had, glancing around for a quick exit should it be needed. "We're not a couple, if that's what you mean. She's my friend, my oldest friend. I've known her for my entire six hundred years, give or take a decade. But we're not romantic, because ew."

Hildegarde narrowed her eyes at me. "Do you dislike women?"

"You mean why am I not trying to woo Camio? She's like a sister to me. I don't have a problem with the female human form itself. The breasts look fun. Now, the male form? It's downright depressing. There's hair where you least expect it, and everything flops around and makes it difficult to sit, and the smells! The smells alone threaten to bring me to my knees, and I'd never inflict that on an intimate partner. Not even for a chance at fun female breasts."

"The fact remains that you have been consorting with a denizen of Abaddon, a demon who serves one of the princes. That is not at all allowed. If you choose to remain in the Court, your relationship—such as it is—with the demon must come to an end. I will not have it said that the Court supports anything to do with Abaddon."

I could swear she sniffed at the end of the statement.

"There was that time that the Court got involved with the vampire kings who tried to take down the demon lords—" I started to point out, but she stopped me with another one of her scary looks.

"We do not support anyone with ties to Abaddon," she said in a louder tone. "It is a well-known rule, and not one that I will allow you to violate. The choice is yours, however. You may remain if you wish, but it has become clear to me that the Fates have something else in mind for you rather than the life of a humble sprite. You may have until sext tomorrow to make a decision about which path you wish to take."

Humility is so not me. And I couldn't deny that it was an intriguing idea that somewhere, there was a better existence just waiting for me to discover it. "Something else like a chivalric tale? I'm not really looking for a woman, but I like the idea of having dashing adventures and daring escapades."

She brushed a spot of dirt off her surcoat. "The vision I had did not speak of what goal you sought, only that you were at a crossroads and must choose a path. I feel obligated to share that knowledge with you, since your constant antics indicate your unhappiness with life here at the Court."

I considered protesting my unhappiness, but when I thought about it, I had to admit she had a point. I'd been at the Court since my mother died at my birth, and although I'd never met her, everyone here seemed to expect that I'd be just like her.

I so was not like her.

But did that mean I was willing to leave the Court? The answer was there even before the thought finished forming. Who could refuse the life of excitement when the only other option was boring spritedom? I'd definitely take Hildegarde up on her offer to head out on my own, and wondered if the other sprites would throw me a leaving party with the strawberry cakes I loved so much.

"Hey," I said, suspicion dawning suddenly. "You wouldn't be trying to get rid of me, would you? It's because of that note I put in the suggestion chest, isn't it? It wasn't aimed at you, I swear. The uprising of lesser sprites, cherubs, and powers who tried to kick you out of the Court was just an unfortunate coincidence. I didn't have anything to do with them. Much. Sure, I painted a few signs and designed a couple of protest tunics, and yeah, I was part of the march on your tower, but I didn't set fire to the internal staircase. All I did was try to light a wall torch. It's a shame the whole tower burned. Er ... did I say happy anniversary? Running the Court for three hundred years is a pretty slick achievement."

"Sext," was all she replied, but the word shot from between clenched teeth with the velocity of a behemoth on a catapult.

I took another step back, covertly checking myself to make sure she hadn't done anything beyond sending me a glare so potent that it would have dropped me if I'd been mortal, and watched silently as she marched off, her hair streaming behind her.

A couple of hours later, I sat in a small room off the cherubs' dormitory, the quietest spot I could find. I rubbed my chin with the feather on a new quill for a few minutes while I thought about what I was going to say, then ran a hand over the vellum to make sure I had suitably scraped it.

Greetings to my friendful Camio.

I hope this missive finds you well. Or, you know, as well as you can be, considering you live and work in Abaddon, and your boss is an actual prince of evil bent on bringing the mortal world to its knees in anguished supplication. I'd like to insert a statement here about my own boss being mean, but I have a feeling that any message I send out will be examined what with the whole fiasco involving Hildegarde's tower burning, and losing all the documents of her reign, and the way the uprising sprites and cherubs ratted me out.

So! Hilders mentioned today that she thinks I have great things in my future. Really big things like adventures and romance and daring acts and all that shite. She's going to de-sprite me so I can go be the best me ever, and I'm thinking it's time to try out some of the dog forms I mentioned in my last letter.

Since I'm going to be at a loose end for a bit, I thought we could meet and spend some time together. I don't mind if it's in *Abaddon, if you can't leave. You know me—I'm fine with demonkind.*

Let me know what you think, and what entrance to Abaddon you want to meet at. And which dog form you think I should have.

Kisses,
Jim

DAY 161
Harvest Time

"My lord." Camio, my best friend since baby sprite-hood, made the sort of bow where you basically kiss your knees, a full-on bow with hints of genuflecting around the hips.

Given that she was currently in a female human form—Cam favored girl forms, not being at all distracted by her upper story—the bow was impressive. Enough that I decided not to let the Court down, even though I'd been out of it for almost half a year. "May I present to you Effrijim, the one who was recommended to you."

A man with the short hair and bare face of the recent Norman invaders stopped in front of us, shooting Camio a sharp glance, one that had her flinching. "Recommended?"

"Aye, my lord Ariton thought you would enjoy adding this one to your legions. Effrijim is free of all ties and bonds, and I do fervently swear he is known for his tenacity, dedication, and cunning."

The demon lord's look became sharper when he snapped out, "Who are you?"

"Camio, my lord," she answered, making another of those knee-kissing bows. "Member of the seventh legion, and faithful servant of your brother, Lord Ariton."

"Ah. Yes. So this is the demon no one has claimed. Ariton said something about finding one, but not wanting it." Amaymon eyed me. He was half a head shorter than Camio, fairly broad across the chest and belly, with the skinny legs of a man who didn't do much but storm around his palace. "Its appearance is not impressive."

I tried to square my shoulders, but it was difficult, since my dog form was currently a low-slung rabbit-hunting model with powerful legs, but with a distinct lack of height. "I am happy to change to a different dog, if you like. I'm trying out a bunch to see what feels right, but if there's something in the hound or lurcher range that you like, I'm all ears. Well, not all ears—"

He interrupted me in the middle of my ear joke by curling his upper lip and gesturing toward me, before striding past, followed by four wrath demons. "It can join the twelfth legion. See to it."

"Is that a good legion?" I asked when the wrathies marched past, scattering scornful looks hither and yon. Wrath demons always did act like their shite smelled like flowers, which was ridiculous, because everyone knew demons smelled only like a nasty, oily smoke. "Like, one that sees a lot of action? Because I was promised all sorts of adventure and thrilling times if I took chances."

"Dammit, Jim!" Camio choked, and hauled me backward at the same time she murmured a bunch of platitudes. She waited until everyone was out of earshot; then she grabbed my little front legs and more or less shook me. "I'm a demon, not your keeper. You need to be more circumspect if you want to be here. The most important rule, which I have told you three times now, is that you can't speak to the princes like that! Fires of Abaddon, why did I ever let you talk me into joining our ranks? This is going to end up with you dying horribly, I know it will."

She'd let go of my legs as she spoke, sinking to the floor of Amaymon's palace deep in Abaddon, and grasping her head like she was going to pull out all her hair.

"Yeah, this form just isn't doing it for me, either." I thought for a moment, then decided I'd go back to the greyhound form I'd used to travel most of the way from the south of Scotland to London. "I'll go with this one. It's pretty good, and I need something that I can live with if Amaymon doesn't let me change forms often. Hey, you have a pain in your head or something?"

"I have a pain in my arse, and its name is Effrijim," she said, but smiled when I sat next to her and leaned against her. She sighed, and leaned into me, too, one arm around me. "Your form is not what I'm concerned about, and you know it."

"Nothing is as important as getting your form right," I said, looking with satisfaction at my long legs. This breed of dog was definitely an improvement. I looked up to catch an expression of concern in Cam's eyes and butted my head against her leg. "You know better than to worry about me. I always land on my feet. That's the one benefit of being my parents' child."

She covered her eyes and gave a brief shudder. "By Saint Peter's thumbs, I can't imagine what Parisi would have thought of you becoming part of Abaddon."

"Eh. Everyone says my mother was goodness personified. Also, you forgot about my father," I reminded her, peering over my shoulder. The tail on this form was nice, but felt a bit lightweight now that I wasn't traveling. I needed a form with more substance. "Maybe I should tell your boss who he was?"

Camio seemed to go pale at the thought. "Fires of Ab—you wouldn't! Jim, swear to me that you will never mention your father to anyone in Abaddon."

"Why?" I asked, scratching behind my left ear. I wondered if I'd picked up fleas from somewhere. "He's one of the men who started the whole shebang. That has to be worth something."

She breathed heavily at me for a few seconds. "Considering your father almost single-handedly destroyed Abaddon in his desire to be with your mother, the only thing your connection will bring you is endless torment. The demon lords have long memories, Jim. Three of them were with your father when Abaddon was formed. They will not ever forget how he tried to obliterate them and it just to be with the Sovereign."

I thought of rolling my eyes, but decided that look did not fit my current face. "Fine, I won't say anything. I'd much rather earn all the honors and accolades on my own, anyway."

"Honors?" She stared at me with eyes that almost bulged out. "Accolades? Oh, Jim, what have we done? This is ludicrous! You're a sprite."

"Former sprite. One that has a great future in front of him, but who has to go through lots of peril and stuff like that. Hildegarde said so. You don't get more peril and possible death than working for a demon lord, eh? What I can't figure out is why your lord wouldn't let me join your group. Is he against dogs?"

"Despite your father, you don't know the first thing about being a demon," she continued, like I hadn't spoken, although her voice was strained with stifled laughter. "You're going to end up either running the place or dead within a week."

"I'd pick the former, but, eh." I wrinkled my nose, wondering how that looked. I had a whole new face to try out expressions. "I'm happy being the dashing demon. So what happens now? Because I just changed forms, which means I'm not under Amaymon's thrall, or spell, or whatever it is they do to keep all the legions in line."

She sighed heavily, kissed me on the top of my head, and got to her feet. "Why you feel this of all paths is the one to lead to your happiness is beyond me, but since it is the choice you have made, I will do everything I can to make the transition from your former location to Abaddon as painless as possible."

I followed when she led me through the corridors in Amaymon's palace, built of black stone into which runes had been set, and lectured me about how to behave around the princes who ruled Abaddon, their elite guards (the wrath demons), and all six classes of demons who served the individual lords.

"You'll start out as a demon sixth class, since you are coming in as a non-Abaddon recruit." We wound our way through a narrow cobbled street that led from the palace to a number of outbuildings, dodging demons running hither and yon, a variety of livestock being herded amongst a number of crude pens, and a bunch of horses wearing black-and-silver barding. "The twelfth legion is always the support legion, so I can't imagine it would be any different for Lord Amaymon. You must swear fealty to him, and after you've done that, you will become a demon."

"Got it. Can do."

She stopped and gently buffeted my shoulder. "And after that, there's no going back. So, for the love of Saint Peter, make sure you want to do this, because once you swear your oath, you'll be a demon to the end of your days."

"I got this," I reassured her, lifting my nose to follow a particularly succulent smell of roasting ox. "Yum! I get to work in the kitchen? Sweet!"

"There is nothing sweet about Abaddon. Oh, Jim. Are you sure? Are you really sure? This is a life of indenturedom and servitude, neither of which you've embraced." She held my head in both her hands, her fingers rubbing the always-itchy spot behind my now-greyhound ears. I gave her a quick lick on the cheek before cocking an eyebrow at her doubt. "I would not for the world want you unhappy. You are dearer to me than even the sun in the heavens."

"Love you, too, sweeting. And you know me better than anyone—I'm not the type to cause trouble or draw attention. I'll be fine, although I appreciate your concern. I swear I won't tell anyone about my parents. Ever. Besides, I'll have you to guide me if I have questions, right? Let's get to the kitchen before they send that roast ox up to Amaymon. I hope they have crackly bits. I love the crackly bits! Maybe they have more than one ox going. I could eat a leviathan and still have room left over for some bread pudding."

That's how it started. One minute I was a hungry and footsore former sprite, and the next I was a demon bound to Amaymon, and part of a legion responsible for domestic stuff. I had a feeling Camio had somehow worked my position into that particular legion, since it was one that seldom ran into any of the top demons, let alone Amaymon himself.

DAY 364,702
18 June 2000

"You know what to do?"

"Yes, of course I know what to do," Ariton, the fourth prince of Abaddon—and Camio's boss—almost snarled at his brother. "It is my plan, after all. Have you secured the leviathan?"

Amaymon, who was sitting on his black crystal throne with his fingers steepled, and fingertips lightly resting on his lower lip (he'd seen that in a movie a few years ago, and it became his main go-to gesture when trying to intimidate people), gave his brother a look that could have curdled fresh milk. "No, I thought I would let it run amok in my halls. Of course it's secured. Where did you put it?"

The last question was asked of me. Camio and I lurked in the background, as was proper for demons. But when Amaymon's attention turned to me, I moseyed forward, one part of my brain distracted by my red legs. I'd been in the form of a pharaoh hound for only a few hours and was still getting used to it. "Yes, your unholy misery. I tucked it away in your oratory, since he said he was bored and wanted something to do."

Amaymon's gaze shifted to me, the act almost knocking me backward with the force of his power. Sharp stabs of pain immediately followed. "A normal demon would place a behemoth in the oubliette."

I ignored the pain that was still lashing me, and smiled, hoping it looked nice on this new, narrower face. "Yeah, but you know how leviathans can be when they get bored; they go deep into revenge pooping, and that's nothing anyone needs to see. Or clean up. Especially clean up. That's why I popped Barry into your oratory so he can watch YouTube."

"Barry?" Amaymon looked more annoyed than a moment ago. "YouTube?"

"Well, I think he's actually looking at some porn site, but I figured it sounds better if I say YouTube," I explained. Behind me, I could hear Camio sucking in her breath like she wanted to tell me off, but couldn't because our bosses were right there. "So, yeah, Barry's tucked away, ready for you to unleash him on Bael."

"Silence!" Amaymon bellowed, turning to Camio. "You, this demon is your responsibility. If anything falls afoul of my plan—"

"Our plan," Ariton interrupted, his upper lip doing the same scorn thing that his brother's always did when he looked at me.

"*I* thought of the leviathan," Amaymon snapped, his gaze at last off me. I took a deep breath, relishing the ability to breathe again.

"Actually, I suggested—" Before I could finish, Camio grabbed my tail, giving it a hard pinch. "Ow!"

"That is a minor point of the plan," Ariton said, waving away the idea with a gesture that said much. "I made the important decisions. After all, I was the one who thought of using the party."

I was going to point out that I had thought of a way for Amaymon and his brother to topple Bael from his position of power as premiere prince of Abaddon, but Camio grabbed me by a bit of frayed rope that served as a collar and hauled me backward to the doors.

The ballroom—where Amaymon had his throne—was empty of everyone but the four of us. Neither demon lord noticed us, because they were too busy arguing over which of them had ownership of the plot to off Bael.

"Jim!" Camio said on a gasping breath once the ballroom doors closed behind us. "You will be the death of me! Of us both! After a thousand years of being in Amaymon's service—"

"Nine ninety-seven, actually," I corrected her. "I'm thinking of having one of those giant cakes with people hiding inside for the big thousand-year party."

"After all that time of being in service, you still haven't learned how to speak properly." She sank down onto one of the chairs that lined the hall, her shoulders slumping. "There are days when I regret ever introducing you to Lord Amaymon."

"Eh," I said, sitting carefully next to her (wasn't sure how this new body's package would do with such an action, since several of my previous dog forms made sitting problematic). I nudged her leg. "You loves me, though, right?"

"Of course," she said, patting me on the head. I turned a bit so her hand would hit the ever-itchy spot behind my ears.

She scratched while my toes clenched in pleasure, and added, "I have always been, and always will be, your friend, Jim. But you simply must learn some humility, or else things could go bad for you."

"Amaymon is all talk and no stabby-stab," I said after quickly looking around to make sure no one could overhear us. "I have his number, don't worry."

"Just be careful, that's all I'm saying," she said, giving me another pat before she got to her feet, obviously waiting for her demon lord to finish up his bitchfest with Amaymon. "I don't think I could be easy in my mind if Lord Amaymon destroyed you. Not that you don't tempt me to smite you at least once a month, but that's an entirely different subject."

"You're a demon first class, not a wrathie yet, chicky," I reminded her, and was going in for a quick rub of my head on her leg, but just then the doors to the ballroom were flung open with enough force to send splinters flying through the air.

Camio snapped to attention and immediately bowed as her boss stormed past her, trailing oaths. She slid me a fast glance out of the side of her eyes, obviously a warning. I mouthed, "Love you, too!" to her, since I knew she'd be seriously pissed if I said that in the hearing of her lord. The widening of her eyes was her only response, but I was happy that even when she was so worried about me, I could prove to her that all was well.

A couple of days later, things went pear-shaped.

ME

Hey, babe. How's life over there in Ariton-land? Everything copacetic? I might not be able to make it to dinner next Friday—something's happened here and I'm not sure I can meet you. Unless you can pop into the mortal world?

CAMIO

Fires of Abaddon! I knew it! I just knew that something would happen, and Lord Amaymon would destroy you, and now look where we are—smack-dab in trouble. Wait, you're OK? You must be all right if you can text me. What happened? Why are you in the mortal world?

ME

I didn't do anything. It wasn't my fault in the least. I told everyone what Barry was doing, but other than Amaymon getting his knickers in a twist because I let a leviathan into his oratory, no one listened to me. No one ever does! I tell you, it's almost enough to give a demon a complex.

CAMIO

For the love of the eight princes, what did you do? No, don't tell me you weren't involved, because I know you had to be. You always are. What happened, Jim?

ME

Barry … uh … he got into Amaymon's personal chambers.

CAMIO

That's annoying, but surely not enough to merit more than a mild punishment? And certainly not enough to scare me with your text. I had to step out of a presentation Lord Ariton was giving on a software company he wants us to run.

ME

As it happens, Barry was in a bit of a mood when he somehow ended up in Amaymon's bedroom rather than the one that Bael will be using tomorrow when he visits for the yearly inspection.

CAMIO

What sort of mood? Was he angry? Did he destroy Lord Amaymon's possessions?

ME

He was … you know … that way.

CAMIO

What? Jim, I don't have time for this. I can see Lord Ariton marching around the conference table, and he only does that when he's agitated. What is the problem?

ME

He was horny, OK? You know I don't like saying that word. Barry spent the last day watching a bunch of bad porn online, and then when he went to the wrong room—I swear I escorted him to the guest chambers—and Amaymon arrived later all hopped-up on his evil plans, well … yeah. Not gonna spell it out.

CAMIO

!!!

CAMIO

I'm calling you. Stay right where you are.

I made a face at where my phone lay on the floor of a dark storeroom (it was infinitely easier to use a pencil, or at worst a toenail, to type when the phone was braced against an object), answering it when it rang a few seconds later.

"I can't believe what you've done, Jim! This is serious! No, don't try to tell me you did nothing wrong."

"I didn't," I said, then sucked a tooth obnoxiously loud. "OK, I ended up doing something that has Amaymon in a mood, but it's not my fault. I listened to what one of the other demons told me to do, and that was a leviathan-sized mistake."

"Just like all the other things you've done over the centuries are mistakes …" She sounded choked for a second, but I couldn't tell if it was laughter or frustration. I was pretty sure it was laughter. "I'm not bound to Amaymon's legions, and yet I know your supervisor almost better than my own."

"Yeah, but he's got the hots for you, so he's always willing to look the other way when something goes wonky for me," I pointed out.

"It doesn't matter. You simply have to ... I'm sorry, my lord." The sound became a bit muffled. I figured Cam must have whipped her phone behind her back so her boss didn't see it, since I could hear a rumble of a man's voice, but his words weren't intelligible. "No, of course not. Nothing is more important than attending to your every word. I was simply speaking to one of Lord Amaymon's minions about the leviathan ... oh. He called ... yes, I agree, it was a terrible event, and I'm sure that an investigation ... with all respect, my lord, perhaps your brother has misunderstood Effrijim's role in—no, my lord. I have known him for more than sixteen hundred years. He's not at all the type to do anything untoward. Well ... yes, I did recommend him, but ... no, my lord. Of course, my lord. No, no, please, Lord Ariton, I humbly beg—"

The phone went silent.

I frowned. "Camio? Babe? Is your boss pissed? Man, I feel all shades of guilty now. Last thing I'd ever want is to get you in bad with Ariton."

More silence filled my ear.

I listened hard, but couldn't even hear the distant sound of voices. Panic had my belly feeling like it was doing somersaults.

"Camio? Did they take your phone? Cam?"

I had to go outside because I thought I might ralph right there in the McDonald's. It took me a good fifteen minutes before I found a demon who would answer my call.

"What do you want?" a gruff voice asked when I took a few deep breaths to settle my stomach.

"Hey, Vodstoc, buddy," I said, trying to sound a whole lot more cheerful than I was. "Haven't seen you since the boss had that company retreat and you cracked your head on one of the trust falls. Long time no chat."

"It was you who let me fall!" Vodstoc snarled, and I figured I'd better placate him since I was fast running out of demons who would talk to me. "I had a scar on the back of my head from it until I was able to change my form."

"And it all worked out in the end, because you love this new form, right? Hey, can you do me a big one and pop over to Ariton's palace, and ask if anyone's seen a demon first class named Camio? She's not responding."

Vodstoc snorted. Actually snorted. Who does that? "Haven't you done enough?"

"What?" I asked, looking at my reflection on the phone screen. Raised eyebrows looked funny with this face.

"I refer to your interference with the leviathan."

"Oh, that." I pursed my lips. Nope. Still not a good look. I'd have to change to another dog form. "Is Amaymon still pissed?"

"'Pissed' is an understatement. Very well, I will agree to your request, but only because I will take any excuse to leave the palace for a bit. I'll ask about Camio."

He hung up before I could find out how things were going in the six hours since I'd been given the boot, but called back within the hour.

"Looks like she's gone," he said, his voice thick with satisfaction.

Fire seemed to burn in my gut, but I ignored it. "Gone? As in left Abaddon?"

"Gone as in evidently Ariton smote her on the spot for letting the rutting beast loose into the master's chambers."

"But she didn't do anything!" I felt like I was standing in the middle of a bonfire. "She wasn't even in Amaymon's palace."

"I'm just reporting what's being said here. It's a bit odd, considering that we all know you were the one to put the leviathan in Amaymon's room."

There had to be something I could do. Someone I could contact. Ariton couldn't just smite Camio on the spot for something she didn't do.

Guilt joined the belly fire, making me get a bit barfy again. "It was a mix-up," I said, thinking madly. Part of me wanted to sit right down and cry with the idea that Cam was gone, but the other part wanted to do something. Now! "Someone gave me the wrong information."

"Shifting the blame is a new low, Effrijim. Why else would Amaymon kick you out of the legions and exile you from Abaddon if you weren't the one who caused the … incident?"

"Are …" I swallowed hard a couple of times. "Are they sure Camio was destroyed? Not imprisoned?"

"The steward I talked to said it was outright destruction. Nothing left of her at all. Guess she had it coming, although we're the ones who have to live with the results of Lord Amaymon's fury."

I sat down, my form shifting to that of a dachshund. I felt about as low as its belly.

"You still there?" Vodstoc asked.

I couldn't say anything. Who knew wiener dogs had throats that seemed to close up with a big lump when they wanted to talk?

"OK, then. You're welcome." Vodstoc's voice was full of sarcasm.

"Thanks," I managed to say, slumping to the ground next to the phone. I needed help. I needed someone who could do what I couldn't. A necromancer to raise Cam's spirit? A vespillo to find her essence? I had to do something, but I was just a demon sixth class.

The mental image came forward, that of Camio laughing a few centuries ago when we got a day off at the same time, and we went to the park to have a picnic. It was one of the happiest days of my life.

Someone had to help me. Someone …

"Thanks," I repeated, getting to my feet. "I don't know what to do, but I know someone who does."

"Huh? Never mind, I don't want to be involved in any of your escapades. Later." Vodstoc hung up, and I sat looking at nothing while I thought, pushing away all the painful emotions.

I'd face that later. Not now.

It just hurt too much now.

THE LIFE AND FABULOUS TIMES OF ME: SALLY, SOVEREIGN, BOSS BABE, AND BEARER OF THE CHALICE OF PARISI
20 June

"Terrin, darling," I said to the man himself as he sat glued to his chair, a mountain of papers in six stacks of varying heights and levels of tidiness splayed out in front of him.

"Hmm?" he asked, not bothering to look up from his laptop. "Is there something you need, Sally?"

The nearest stack of papers quivered, just as if a sneeze would send them into an explosion of papery chaos.

I eyed the stack.

"No," he said, an obvious warning in his voice.

I tsked and propped myself up on the unoccupied corner of his desk. "You know I love you to the ends of the earth and back, but, sugar, you can be such a wet blanket. Also, you understand me far too well for my comfort. But that matters not. Do you know a demon named"—I consulted my phone—"Effrijim? Apparently, it used to be with Amaymon, but was forcibly removed from Abaddon for some hullabaloo over a leviathan with romance on his mind."

"Effrijim?" He looked up at the name, his brown eyes, brown hair, and general appearance of mildness making him look innocuous, naive, and possessed of a bovine level of intelligence, none of which was true. Quite the opposite, as a matter of fact, and once again I prided myself on picking the perfect partner with whom to run the Court.

"That's the name," I said, glancing at the text message again.

"There was a sprite named Effrijim who I seem to recall causing issues with our predecessor," he said after a moment's obvious dig through his (prodigious) memory. "I didn't meet him myself, but the name is somewhat familiar. I believe there are some records concerning him that I can look up, if you like."

"That little … he was a sprite?" I considered pursing my lips, but as a dedicated alumnus of the Carrie Fay Academy of Really Nice Hair and Perky Bosoms, I confined myself to a raised eyebrow, instead. "He didn't say anything about that. He's a demon now."

"It's a demon," Terrin corrected, his attention back to the paperwork he loved so dearly. It was one of the reasons why we as Sovereign had ruled so successfully for the last seven hundred years. "Demons use the 'it' pronoun."

"Oh, I don't think that's going to fly these days," I answered, still thinking about the demon. While I was naturally shocked and horrified that anyone would leave the Court, the idea of rubbing shoulders with all those demons and demon lords had a strange appeal to it.

Terrin paused for a moment. "I didn't think of that, but you're right. What with all the social justice and such, I'm a bit surprised the demons haven't demanded new pronouns. Or are they happy with gender-neutral, do you think?"

"Sugar, much though I love keeping my fingers on the pulse of the Court, that power sadly does not extend to Abaddon." Of their own accord, my lips pursed for a scant moment. "But that doesn't have to remain the case."

"What does Effrijim want?" Terrin asked, tapping away on the keyboard.

"If there was a way I could slip in … a very strong glamour would be needed to hide my Court ties, of course … but that wouldn't be difficult to arrange. No, the problem is the surplus of demon lords. … Hmm? The demon Effrijim wants revenge."

"Demons," Terrin muttered in a dismissive tone.

"No, no, you have it wrong. He doesn't want revenge against a mortal, or even an immortal; he wants revenge against Ariton."

That had Terrin looking up, a question in his eyes.

"I don't know, exactly," I answered the question, holding up my phone. "He just asked if I could help him exact revenge against Ariton."

"Please tell me you're not considering it," Terrin said, a somewhat fatalistic expression settling on his face.

"Of course I'm considering it. We're the Sovereign. It is our sworn duty to aid, assist, and abet denizens of the Otherworld, and as Effrijim has been removed from Abaddon, he falls under that umbrella."

"And the fact that you've been itching for a reason to dip your toes into Abaddon waters has nothing to do with your sudden willingness to help a stranger, does it?" Terrin asked, once again piercing straight through to the heart of my soul.

I gave him my best Carrie Fay smile.

The one with all the teeth.

"Sugar, I've said it before, and I'll say it again: We could bring Abaddon to the modern age and peak efficiency if they'd just name me as premiere prince. I have a comprehensive, forty-five-day plan to take that place from downright medieval to prosperous and thriving."

"The last thing that I want to see is a thriving, efficient Abaddon," Terrin said in the same warning tone he'd used earlier. "The very thought of it scares the peawadding out of me."

"What, exactly, is a peawadding?" I couldn't help but ask. "Is it something naughty? Risqué? Do I want one?"

He sighed. "What are you going to do about the demon?"

"Help him, of course." I wiggled my shoulders. "He used to be a sprite, after all."

Terrin murmured something about knowing better than to try to stop me when I had my heart set on an action. I just blew him a kiss and trotted off to attend to a little pressing business.

I had a feeling I was going to enjoy what was coming.

23 June

"You do know that's full of fat and sugars and preservatives that are not healthy." I nodded to the ice cream cone I held at arm's length, careful to keep out of the splash zone.

"Yeah, but a demon's gotta eat, and since that ice cream dude is the only one open in the park, I'll take my chances with a little delicious, silky smooth, nearly orgasmic berries and cream. Can you tip it a little away from me so I can get a good lick ... perfect."

"What is it—other than unhealthy carbohydrates—you want from me?" I asked, more than a little amused by the avidity with which the demon ate the ice cream. He appeared in the form of a Great Dane dog, evidently a canine being his preferred form.

He delicately plucked the remaining cone from my fingers, crunched loudly for a minute, then sat down and licked his lips a few times to catch any stray crumbs or ice cream. "I want Ariton to go away. Destroyed would be preferable, but I'd settle for banished to the Akasha where he can't ever get out to squash innocent demons. You can do that, right? Banish demon lords?"

I drew out an antiseptic wipe and dabbed at my fingers. Carrie Fay had many things to say about the state of one's manicure, and none of them involved either melted ice cream or dog slobber. "Given the correct tools, yes."

"Tools?" Effrijim sucked a tooth. "What sort of tools? Like power tools? You going to table saw Ariton's head off? I want to watch if you do."

"Gruesome," I said, smiling. "I approve of this attitude. The tools I'm thinking of are not available ... yet. But I can see where they might be, given the right set of circumstances."

"So you'll do it?" Effrijim asked, his ears pricking up.

"I shouldn't," I said hesitantly, wondering how I was going to spin the plan that was slowly coming to mind.

"Yeah, but when have you let that stop you?"

I ceased musing and cocked an eyebrow.

The demon gave a doggy cough and managed to arrange his expression into one of contrite regret. "That is, what couldn't you do if you put your impressive and limitless mind to it?"

"Nice save," I said with a nod. "Very well. I am inclined to help you because, for one, I am the bearer of the Chalice of Parisi. I assume you know it well."

Effrijim wrinkled his muzzle. "My mom's favorite cup? Yeah, I know it. I take it you looked up the incidents in my past?"

"And a colorful three volumes they were, yes," I answered, wondering what it would take to get Terrin to let me go on vacation for a year or two. "But then, I'd expect the child of the Sovereign and one of the dark lords who founded Abaddon would be a bit quirky. However, that is only part of the reason I've decided to give you aid. According to my predecessors, you have a role to play in events important to the Otherworld."

"I do?" Effrijim squawked, then cleared his throat and spoke in a more natural tone. "I mean, yeah, of course I'm all up in important stuff and things, but hey, you want to fill me in on just what I'm going to be doing? Because Hilders never came right out with whatever it is, and why I had to leave the Court when I did."

"I have no idea," I said, plucking a stray hair from my sleeve. I'd decided to wear my favorite bright red power suit to the meeting, since it always made me feel especially wicked, and what better emotion was there when dealing with demons? "Many of the records from that time burned in a mysterious fire. What remains speaks of many, many discussions about behavior."

Effrijim made what I can only describe as a moue. "Yeah, about that ... Hildie really had a thing for everyone following the rules to the letter, and I'm not a 'rules to the letter' sort of guy. I'm more of a free spirit. Not beholden to anyone. A loner who doesn't need anyone—except when it comes to dealing with demon lords—and who's untouched by drama."

I leaned down to meet his gaze. His eyes grew huge when I said softly, "And yet, sorrow is wrapped so deep around you I can see its stain leaching out to your soul. The fact that you, a demon, have a soul is in itself a contradiction, but regardless, your pain is palpable."

He sucked in a breath, and for an instant, the light in his eyes dimmed, but his head snapped up as he gave me a long look. "I just want revenge, OK?"

"You know, sugar, I am many things, but stupid isn't one of them. It's clear that you've suffered a grievous loss, and you want to strike back in return. The question is, how far are you willing to go to obtain that revenge?"

"Whatever it takes," he answered, his voice oddly flat before he cleared his throat and continued in a normal tone. "I'm all over revenge, babe. If I can help you with anything to make that happen, then I'll do it."

"Very well." I thought for a moment. "I don't normally indulge in the visions that my predecessors relied on for insight, but I will see to it that you are set onto the path that will lead—if you take it—to the revenge you seek. Be warned, demon Effrijim, that result may not happen anytime soon. Several pieces need to fall into place, and I'm not entirely sure they will do so. Unfortunately, my better half will not let me manipulate things outright, which is just enraging, don't you think? What's the point of being half of the Sovereign if you aren't allowed to fix things? But Terrin insists that we give everyone the ability to make their own choices and respect their free will. It's all poppycock, of course, but I live to make Terrin happy, so I do as he insists."

The dog blinked at me a couple of times. "Gotcha. What happens now?"

"Now," I said, standing up and dusting off ice-cream-cone crumbs from my front. I made a mental note to do a bit of snooping around Abaddon. I'd need a culpable demon lord if my plan was to bear fruit. "You survive."

"Yeah, but what—"

I returned to the Court before the demon could finish his question, the grass of the park changing underfoot to black-and-white tile as I strode down the hall of the administrative wing of our main building, pausing to poke my head into Terrin's office. "Sugar, do you remember a demon lord who used to abide in the mortal world about eighty or so years ago? He made some sort of splash in the silent-movie scene."

Terrin was clearly dealing with some issue or other with a cherub who perched opposite him on the edge of a hard wooden chair. When he glanced up at my question, his forehead was furrowed. "I believe so. I think you're right that he was a silent-film star." He offered a name that had me nodding.

"That's the one. What was his real name?"

He thought for a moment. "I believe it's Magoth," he finally said. "I can look it up if it's important."

"It's not at all necessary, sweet one. That's the demon lord I was thinking of. You are the best seneschal in all the Otherworld," I told him, blowing a kiss, and casting a glance toward the cherub before looking back at him.

He gave a slight shake of his head, which let me know I wasn't needed to deal with this particular problem.

I headed off to my office, planning many things, but most of all, I started to pull together in my mind the sort of industrial-strength glamour I was going to need in order to get by undetected in Abaddon.

DAY 366,162
19 June 2004

"And, I'm like, it's been four years! They said they'd help me with my big project four years ago, but there's been nada coming out of the Court in all that time. You'd think four years would be enough to get things kicked into high, wouldn't you?" I took a big slurp of coffee (heavy on the cream and sugar, because a demon has to keep his strength up). "I mean, you go to all the trouble to locate this very important person whose name I can't tell you, and get them to say they'll help you, and then blammo. Radio silence for four years. Four years!"

Oblitton, one of my coworkers, who was also a troll with tendencies toward kleptomania, sidled away and murmured, "It's a shame, it's definitely a shame. Uh. I have to get back to the phones. You know how Sam is."

I dropped my now-empty cup into the sink, pretending not to hear the crack of ceramic hitting the metal sink. "How someone as powerful as the important person whose name I can't tell you can loll around for four years—four!—doing nothing while I'm waiting for vengeance is beyond me."

Oblitton slipped into his cubicle and immediately slapped on his headset.

I stood outside my cubicle, wondering if I'd been wrong to put my trust in Sally. I thought for a moment of Camio, my spirits sinking until I felt the urge to go sit in a closet and cry.

"Dalmatians don't cry," I told myself, looking down at my spotty legs. I'd tried out the form a few days ago, but already I was finding it lacking. "I just gotta have faith that Sally will do what she said she'd do."

No one else in the office paid me any attention, so with a sigh that I felt down to my toenails, I got back into my seat. "Hi, you've reached Whiskey Sam's Genuine Psychic Guidance Hotline, Jim speaking. How can I help?"

"Yeah, hi, I … um … wait, if you're a psychic, aren't you supposed to know what I want?" The voice was filled with suspicion.

I consulted the script that Sam insisted we follow. Per instructions, I chuckled, which isn't easy when you're in the form of a Dalmatian. I don't know if those dogs just don't have great vocal cords, or if chuckling is alien to them, but the resulting sound wasn't at all mirthful. I made a decision right then and there that just as soon as I had a quiet moment, I'd switch my form to that of a glorious black Newfoundland dog. I'd seen pictures of one earlier, and the sheer magnificence of it blew me away. "I know, right? It seems like I should, but you know how it is with psychic abilities—you don't want to blow all your power on trivial stuff, right? You got to save it for the big guns."

"Oh." The woman on the phone sounded disappointed. "I guess that makes sense. What do I need to tell you?"

"Whatever you want." I nosed the script aside. I never felt comfortable sticking to it, even though Sam said it made life much easier. "What's on your mind?"

"My husband." Her voice had dropped to an intimate level, and I imagined she was glancing around furtively to make sure she wasn't overheard. "I think he's cheating on me, and I need you to tell me if he is."

"Yup," I said, knowing most of the unhappy people who called were likely in relationships that, if not outright abusive, were probably at best dysfunctional. "He sure is."

"How do you know?" Her voice rose as she spoke. "I haven't told you what he's doing!"

"OK, you tell me what he's doing," I said, wanting to point out that she'd called a psychic hotline and was surprised when I acted like I had psychic powers.

Spoiler: I don't.

"Well," she said in the same hushed tone, "it's not just one thing that's suspicious. But he does hide his phone whenever I'm around."

"Cheating," I said, peering around the cubicle wall when one of my coworkers emerged from the entrance with a bag of take-out noms. I sniffed the air a few times. Pad Thai! I loved pad Thai! I eyed Ramon, the coworker, and wondered if he was susceptible to puppy dog eyes. Immediately, my form changed to that of a stunningly handsome Newfoundland dog. One with lots of fur, and big, heart-tugging eyes. I fluttered my eyelashes at Ramon, deciding that this definitely was the right choice of forms. I could just feel how emotive my face was. "He's definitely cheating on you."

"And then there's all the overtime he says he's putting in just so we can take a trip to Disney World before the kids go back to school."

"Cheating," I repeated, leaning out a bit farther until Ramon sent a wary glance my way as he peeled back the lid on the container. I sucked up a bit of drool that started the minute the full blast of pad Thai scent hit my highly effective nose.

"And he keeps mentioning Marjory, his new supervisor, and how clever she is, and how she takes care of herself even though she has three kids and a full-time job, and that I've let myself go. He told me I'm a slob, and that I need to pull my crap together, and that I should be more like Marjory. I have two toddlers under four, and go to school at night, and work from home whenever I can get the kids into a day care program. I don't have time to have massages and personal trainers and chef-made meals like Marjory!"

"Cheating, cheating, cheating," I said, adding out of the side of my mouth to Ramon, "Heya! Where'd you get that? It smells delicious. Does it have any onions or garlic? Dogs can't have those, you know. It messes with them. But that doesn't smell like there's anything bad in it."

Ramon pulled the pad Thai up tight to himself, just like he was protecting it from a ravaging herd of Newfies. I experimented by curling up one black flew at him. The lip curl was incredibly responsive. Newfies rocked!

"Do you really think so?" My attention was yanked back to the caller by the misery evident in her voice. "Is that what your ... er ... spirit guide or whatever tells you?"

"Yup. And Giza—my spirit guide—also says you can do way better than the deadbeat who doesn't appreciate the fact that you run your home, gave him two fabulous kiddos, and still hold down a job. I'm not gonna say to kick your hub to the curb, because only you can make that decision, but, girl, the spirits all agree that you need to get yourself into some counseling so that you can realize you are a queen, and deserve to be treated like one."

"Oh, I … oh." She sounded flustered, but pleased. "They really said that? I'm a queen? Do you mean in a past life?"

"Sure," I said, willing to go with the flow if it got her the help she needed. "Hey, Giza just came through with a couple of phone numbers of people who can help you. The first is a woman's shelter, and the second is a group for women in dicey relationships. Giza says they'll get you onto the path you're supposed to be on, and into the headspace you want. You got a pen?"

I read the phone numbers off the couple of cards I kept hidden under the monitor stand—Sam didn't like us diverting paying customers to services he didn't profit from—and by the time she thanked me for my psychic insights, she sounded happier, chattering about how she always knew she had some role of importance in the past. I felt a momentary twang at that lie, but put my faith in the resources I'd provided.

"They'll do a lot more for her than we can," I told Ramon, who had turned away from me to eat. I slid off my chair and wandered over to him, sniffing deeply. "So! Did you say where you got that from? Is it chicken pad Thai? That's my most favorite food ev—"

I stopped, feeling a bit woozy for a few seconds.

"I am not sharing with a demon," Ramon said, his brows pulled together as he clutched his pad Thai closer. "You can get your own if you want—"

Just as I was shaking my head, hoping the wooziness cleared, everything went swirly for a few seconds; then I found myself standing on a hideous carpet, in a small hotel room, facing a woman with curly hair who was bent out of a window coughing like she was a six-pack-a-day smoker.

I sat down to consider this new situation, not best pleased. Obviously, the woman was a Guardian, and she'd summoned me. I was about to tell her that I didn't have time to conduct the heinous acts she no doubt wanted, because Sally might need my help at any time, but then the Guardian turned around to face me.

Her eyes were hazel, the same as Camio's.

Mind you, the startled expression was all hers, and after she introduced herself—her name was Aisling—she went on and on about how she'd called me there to help her with some project.

I got over the eerie familiarity of her eyes, and decided that the sooner I did whatever it was she wanted, the sooner I'd be available to Sally.

In hindsight, I might have been a bit snarky with her, but by the time we were doing pre-bed walkies, I felt like I had her number.

She was clueless, naive, had no idea what a Guardian was, not to mention didn't know the first thing about demons to the point where I was just about to tell her that I was too busy to help her. However, an hour later (after I partook of a little privacy behind a large azalea bush in the Tuileries), Aisling went into full grumpy mode, and I decided this had to end.

"Tell me you didn't poop behind the flowers," Aisling grumbled as she ducked to avoid an orange tree's outstretched branches and struggling around various small shrubs before stumbling to a stop behind the azalea. She waved a handful of grocery store bags in one hand. "You did! Dammit, Jim, I'm a Guardian, not an acrobat! I get that you can't use a toilet like a normal demon, but can you at least do that where it's easy for me to clean up and I don't get scratched to pieces?"

I paused in midstep, glancing back at her. An echo of a memory lurked at the edge of my mind, a little zing of pain making me wonder.

Just who was this unlearned Guardian? Why did she seem familiar? Was this a sign?

Did I have to poop again?

"Do you know Sally?" I squinted at her, unsure of whether I was facing what I could only think of as a sign from Cam.

Aisling had wildly curly brown hair and a pleasant but perfectly normal face, not the least bit like Camio's long blond braids and pretty heart-shaped face. Their eyes were similar, but that could just be a coincidence.

I gave a mental shake of my head. I was imagining things. What I needed was to simply deal with Aisling as quickly as possible, then get in contact with Sally and ask her how the plan to destroy Ariton was going.

"Me?" Aisling grunted a little as she shoved her way through the back side of the azalea, picking up after me. "No, I don't know a Sally. For the love of Pete, Jim, this is beyond normal for a dog to have this much ... droppings. Is it because you're a demon?"

I spun around, watching her as she finished cleaning up before proceeding to a nearby trash bin that I'd already watered when she wasn't looking.

"No one ever said I was stupid," I said softly when she ranted a little more about some green dragon who had done her wrong.

We walked back to our hotel, her talking nonstop, and me thinking long and hard.

That night, I lay on the blanket and pillow she'd placed on the floor for me, and watched her sleep.

There was something about her, a sense of being lost and alone and needy, that plucked at me. And then there was the fact that when I was with her, the pain of Camio's loss, which felt like lead straps binding me, seemed to ease. Just a bit. But still, it was there.

I got up and marched over to where Aisling had her face smooshed into a pillow, really looking at her. She was as grumpy as the day was long, but she'd also fed me a couple of hamburgers, taken me out every time I needed to go, and even bought me some things at a local pet store, including a nice collar.

No one had ever bought me a collar. Or a brush. Or doggy toothpaste and a toothbrush.

Only Aisling Grey did those things.

"You want me to have healthy teeth," I told her. "You care about me. Camio cared, too. She was always nagging me about stuff just like you do."

She snored slightly, muttered something about a dragon named Drake, and buried her face deeper into the pillow.

"I don't know who you are, but if Cam approves of you, then so do I," I told her. "I guess this is the path that Garders wanted me to take. It just better work. You'll make sure it works, right?"

Aisling snorted, lifted her head an inch, and, without opening her eyes, said in a thick voice, "Sure. Go to sleep."

I nodded at her promise, but hesitated, imagining I could hear Camio, so added, "I won't leave you, then. For one, you have good taste when it comes to the kind of food this magnificent form demands. For another, you need me. Like a lot. I can't think of when I've met a more naive Guardian. So that's it, then. You help me to make Sally's plan happen, and I'll take care of you.

Because it's a tough world out there, babe, and you'll be dragon fodder if I'm not here to keep you safe."

"Mmrf," she murmured into the pillow, followed by another muffled snore.

I nodded again, then went back to my blanket, noticing a sheet of crumpled paper that stuck out from under the bed. I nosed it out and squinted to read it in the dim light. It was a photocopied page of an old grimoire, one that evidently Aisling had used to summon me. Along the top was written: *Here are the pages you asked for. I hope they help! Beth.*

In a different hand, someone else had noted in bright red ink on the edge of the phtotocopy: *Don't worry if you don't have the exact ingredients. It's the intention that matters.*

I eyed that last notation, wondering about it, because ingredients very much do matter when it comes to summoning. The ink on the page was hot pink, just like the phone number written on a scrap of paper that Sally had given me four years ago.

I left the photocopy and returned to my bed, such as it was. I had a lot to think about, but for the first time in four years, the world seemed a bit brighter. Lighter, even. More hopeful.

The following day, when Aisling was having a shower, I dug through my phone until I found an old text entry and launched a new message.

ME

Hiya! Got myself bound to a Guardian. Just an FYI in case you need me to help with whatever thing Hildegarde hinted at. Because it's been four years, and there's been no action. Not that I'm telling you what to do, but if you didn't send this Guardian my way as part of your master plan, let me know. Although at this point, I kind of hate to leave her. I mean, yeah, she's a Guardian, and they're badass, but she seems a bit … needy. Like she is in way over her head. And since she wants me to have good dental hygiene with no gum disease, and lets me have hamburgers with fries even though she said my fantabulous form was a bit chunky, and takes me out whenever I ask, I figured I'd stay and make sure she's OK. Unless that's not your plan. Er … is it?

ME

Sally?

ME

You guys are almost as frustrating as the dragons Aisling keeps making us visit, and they are world-class ignorers of questions. Welp, no news is good news, right? Guess I have a new demon lord. Yell when you need me to help take down Ariton!

DRAGON REVISITED

WHO'S WHO?

This is a different sort of novella in that it takes a long, long look at a much loved character from my dragon books, Drake Vireo. Drake was introduced in YOU SLAY ME, and like the love of his life, Aisling Grey, appears in almost all of the dragon books.

If you're confused as to who Drake is, why a demon named Jim is in the form of a Newfoundland dog (be sure to check Jim's short story, "Becoming Effrijim," for his history), and who this Aisling person is who drives Drake close to breaking, then you'll want to dive into YOU SLAY ME to start your dragon journey.

Because I have a deep and abiding love of Easter eggs, you'll find several here. Feel free to let me know how many you find, and if Drake's history before Aisling explains his actions once he found her.

Smooches!

Katie MacAlister
September 2023

ONE

1 January 1857
We lost Fodor to a storm off Cape Horn. I wish that my ascension to wyvern was not due to the tragedy of losing him, but thus are the vagaries of fate. I will do all I can to protect the sept, and have so sworn.

Henceforth, I am known as Drake Vireo.

Drake sat back, feeling both a sense of sadness and satisfaction he had at last taken up the mantle he was born to assume. He tapped on the journal with the end of the pen, then dipped the nib into the inkwell again.

Addendum: I have decided to keep a journal. As my grandam pointed out, documentation of a modern-thinking wyvern will offer much insight and provide a great benefit to future generations. It is for this reason I will devote an hour each day to noting in this diary such things as are brought to my attention.

Also, Kostya has started one.

30 September 1859
I see it has been more than two years since I decided to keep a journal.

I will do better, beginning with today. I am on the way to see my grandam, who has called me to her side. She says the matter is of some impor—

The carriage in which Drake was riding hit a pothole, sending the quill and traveling ink bottle to the floor. He sighed, and decided he'd fill in the rest of the day's entry after he'd seen Piroska.

A short half hour later, Drake entered the salon lit with sunlight, the noise and scent of the Paris that flowed past his grand-mère's house filling him with a sense of mingled familiarity and unease. The former was due to his having lived there during his early years, while the latter …

"There you are, my Drake. How handsome you look in that suit. Did some woman pick it out?"

The voice that greeted him was as soft as the wind, yet had a thread of steel that Drake was all too familiar with.

He bowed over his grandam Piroska's hand, kissing it before doing the same to each of her slightly perfumed cheeks. "As a matter of fact, a woman did give it to me. A beautiful woman, with green eyes filled with laughter, and a heart bigger than all of the Otherworld."

"Flatterer," Piroska laughed, pinching his arm before smoothing a hand over the lapel of the dragon-weave suit that she'd given him a few weeks earlier. "I would say that the tailor did an exceptional job, but you could wear sackcloth and still look elegant."

He bowed his head in acknowledgment of the compliment, taking a seat next to her and accepting a cup of tea. The conversation for the next six minutes was trivial at best, and Drake wondered if she was going to address the elephant in the room … but perhaps she was unaware of the happenings?

"And now that I have bored you almost to sleep, I must say my piece."

Drake stiffened, carefully setting down his mostly untouched tea. "You've heard?"

"Of course. Did you think that you could dally with four red dragons in defiance of their wyvern without the news of Chuan Ren's demand for reparation? I agree her claim is outrageous—*you* did not force her to remove your sexual partners from her sept—but still, you did have a role in the goings-on."

He hated the feeling of dancing around subjects with his grandmother. He had always spoken openly to her. "It doesn't surprise me that you heard of the situation, but I fail to understand why you are concerned about it. I have explained to Chuan Ren I had no designs on the four members of her sept, and that they came to me willingly and of their own accord. I refused her demands, naturally, and that is the end of it. I regret she took such extreme actions as to kick them out of the sept, but she is their wyvern, not I. I can do nothing."

Grand-mère gave him a long look that had him remembering the time when, as a child, he'd been caught with a plate full of his favorite tarts freshly stolen from the kitchen. He'd received a stern lecture for that particular escapade, and he noted with some amusement that Piroska's tone bore a remarkable likeness to the one she'd had in that incident.

"It is not Chuan Ren and the red dragons that concern me—although really, Drakeling, four women at once? what did three of them do while you were paying attention to the fourth?—but the fact that for some time, you have been unhappy in your romantic life. I am worried about you, *kincsem*. You are not just my wyvern; you are a most cherished grandson, and I would see you happy in your personal life as you are with the sept."

"My personal life is fine," he attempted to reassure her, pushing down deep the pain that threatened to rise up and ruin the moment. "I am happy. Quite happy, now that Chuan Ren has retreated to Hong Kong."

She tapped him on his knee. "Now, that is an untruth. What is it, Drake? What has turned you from seeking a mate to attempting to bed the entire female population of Europe?"

"I am, naturally, loath to tell my beloved grand-mère that she is wrong, but I assure you that I have no such goals. I simply find relationships with women … lacking." He was aware of a faint warmth on his cheeks, and was more than a little amazed that his grandmother so discomfited him he actually blushed. He was a wyvern! Wyverns didn't blush.

Wyverns also didn't have to listen to lectures about their sexual escapades. It was on the tip of his tongue to tell Grand-mère that, but the genuine concern in her brilliant emerald eyes kept the words behind his teeth.

"Lacking how?" she asked.

"Grand-mère," he said, allowing his exasperation to fill his voice. "This is not a subject I care to discuss."

"Of course not. You're male, and every male dragon I've ever met has the same ridiculous notions that they are not subject to emotions, and thus refuse to acknowledge any issues therewith. What do you find lacking about females?"

"You're not going to let this go, are you?" Drake asked with sudden prescience. He thought of putting his foot down and forbidding the discussion, but a lifetime knowledge of his grandmother's character warned him she would not let the subject go, not until she'd had her say. It was better to let her vent her spleen so he could go back to the business of being wyvern. "You're going to continue to pick away at the subject until you break me."

She laughed as she patted his leg. "As if I could do any such thing. You are a strong man, and a stronger wyvern. But that strength does you a disservice when it comes to finding a mate."

"A mate." He couldn't resist filling the last word with scorn. "Given the scarcity of wyverns' mates, I'm not holding my breath to find one."

"And yet, you should," Grand-mère said in a tone that had lost all its gentle teasing. "No, do not give me that look. I did not mean literally, but figuratively. What troubles me is that over the centuries you have gone from dalliances with a female, singular—mortal and immortal—to groups of mortal females, and seldom any dragonkin."

"Since you just lectured me about the wisdom of bedding four red dragons, that subject is clearly moot," he felt obligated to point out.

She waved it away. "From what I've heard, that was an aberration. Am I wrong?"

Drake looked away, not answering.

"And that fact tells me that something is lacking in your life," Grand-mère continued. "Something that drives you to take solace in many shallow relationships with human women rather than searching for one female who will fulfill your needs completely."

"If someone told me that today my grandam would lecture me about my sexual choices, I would have called him mad," Drake said calmly, rising and moving over to glance out of the window. It was raining, dampening his spirits along with the city itself, making him aware of the pain he kept hidden deep, now stirred at Piroska's words. "You are worried unnecessarily, I assure you. Shall we speak of other things? How is Jakab?"

"Why do you think you will not find a mate?" she asked, ignoring his attempt to deflect her.

He spun around to stare at her, wondering if something in his expression or voice had given him away, or if she was simply exhibiting one of the traits that made her so uncanny. "Wyverns' mates are rare. I would be foolish to expect to find one; thus, I take solace in other relationships."

"Trivial ones with mortals," she insisted. "Ones where you are evidently—if what your brother says is true—uncomfortable with just one partner. Kostya told me he went to visit you recently, and when he found you, you were engaged in what appeared to be an extremely spirited session of sexual congress with three women. And now there is this episode with the four red dragons. No, do not glare at me. It is not your fleeting dalliances of which I speak. A mate is something unique, something precious, and a wyvern's mate doubly so. There are not enough of them to go around as it is, and your cavalier attitude toward women—"

"I do not have a cavalier attitude," he interrupted, squaring his shoulders and making a mental note to have a few words in Kostya's ear about tattling private details to their grandmother. "I enjoy women, yes, but that does not have any impact on my ability to lead the sept. And Kostya needs to mind his own business."

"He loves you. He worries—less than I do, that is true, but he sees that in your personal relationships, you are not happy. I'm sure you will consider this forward of me to ask, but I remind you that I am an old lady who has seen more than a millennium of dragons live their lives—are you afraid that there is no mate out there for you, or that you are not worthy of such a woman?"

Drake ignored the question. It was too close to the secret pain, the one that haunted him in the late hours of the night. He'd long learned that the only way to deal with it was to fill his bed with as many women as would reasonably fit, spending his time both providing and taking pleasure until he was too exhausted to think. It was only then that he could sleep without the nagging pain. "The sept will always come first. Always. Yes, it is true that I have many sexual assignations, but that is simply my nature. As you said yourself on many occasions, I am different from most other dragons. Thus, I do not feel bonds to any one female. I never have, and I honestly don't believe it is in me to so honor a mate. It is for that reason that I do not seek one out, and am instead content to live my life with as many 'fleeting dalliances' as I desire."

She said nothing, just watched him.

Drake gave her hand a gentle squeeze. "Since you have spoken so frankly to me, I will do the same. Do not worry about me, Grand-mère. I am simply not meant to be bound to one woman, mate or not. It is not within my nature to live that way. Women are intended to provide men pleasure, and if I partake of what they offer me, it is of no importance. Sex with mortals, especially, is merely a release, a physical necessity to clear the mind. Enjoying a variety of women is as natural to me as breathing, and to do otherwise would put the sept at risk."

"I feel the pain in you, *kincsem*," she said softly, her eyes now somber.

He shook his head. Not even to the person he trusted most would he bare his soul.

"I don't believe I've ever heard a dragon say he was

shtupping as many women as he physically could in order to keep the sept safe," she finally said, adjusting a
pillow to a more comfortable position.

"Grand-mère!" Drake reared back, frowning.
"Shtupping?"

She bobbed her head to the side. "My next-door
neighbor Miriam is Jewish. She has many excellent
insights on her grandsons, and we take much pleasure
talking about life over mahjong in the afternoons. Very
well. You do not wish to confide in me what is causing
you to feel that you are unworthy, or perhaps that it is
hopeless to seek a mate. Just remember that I will do
whatever it takes to ensure your happiness. If you ever
need help, I am here."

"It does not surprise me that the First Dragon has
so honored you by making you a reeve," he said, kissing
her cheeks again before rising. "You are infuriating and
nosy and pushy, and the most wonderful of all dragons.
I love you dearly."

She smiled, one hand caressing his cheek before she
waved him away. "As I do you. Go, then. But remember
my words. I will always be here for you."

He left, one part of him warmed by her obvious
love, but the other part of his soul, the part stained with
shame, tainted the emotion and left him squaring his
shoulders with the now-familiar weight of responsibility.

Perhaps Grand-mère was right and four women at
once was folly. He hadn't particularly enjoyed having
all four of the red dragons dally with him three nights
before, but they had served their purpose in distracting
him from the fear, and that was all that mattered.

Wyverns did not fear.

TWO

24 December 1902

This journal came to my attention this afternoon. I thought I'd lost it, but I found it when sorting through some belongings. I have, again, been remiss in documenting all there is to being a modern wyvern.

There was a sárkány last week. It went as well as could be expected.

Afterward, Kostya emerged from wherever he's been in hiding, proposing that he should go to the weyr and demand they reaccept the black sept. I pointed out that to date, he's found only two black dragons, and since then, one has died in a minor skirmish in Latvia. He has agreed to wait until such time as he has enough members to convince the other wyverns to recognize the sept.

And speaking of him, he mentioned that he discovered he had two children by two mortals, but all four recently died to the bloody flux. He was distraught because he had no idea the women—sisters, as it turns out—bore him children, and he only found out after the landlord of one of them found a note with his information and contacted him to settle their bills and pay for the burials. He said—

Drake looked up when Kostya tapped on his door before opening it. "I'm leaving for Constantinople and thought I would say good-bye while you weren't trying to plow the field of every woman in Buda."

One of the two women who lay asleep next to him, their limbs tangled together, woke at the noise and murmured something sleepily. Drake grabbed at the inkwell on his knee as it started to slip, carefully capping it and placing it on the stand next to him.

Kostya noticed the movement of the quilt, and gave Drake a jaded look.

"Too late," Drake said, more than a little tired of everyone nagging him about the fact that he was simply not meant for one woman, and one woman alone. The sun would never rise on a day when he felt otherwise.

7 August 1914

I found this journal when taking over the London house belonging to my mother. I am greatly remiss with regard to documenting the happenings to the green dragons, but I am determined to rectify that.

My grandam Piroska, her mate—Jakab—and my cousin Dmitri arrived in London last week. Dmitri was his usual surly self, while Jakab has barely removed his nose from the cases of books he's managed to acquire during a short time.

The visit has been pleasant, but I am troubled.

Drake set down the pen, unwilling to put down too much. He considered his options, then, making a quick decision, strode out of his study and down a flight of stairs, and entered the large room his mother had called her library.

"There you are," Piroska said, glancing up as he entered. "You do not approve?"

Jakab sat in a corner surrounded by crates, a large tome on his lap as he read. Drake knew from experience that he would be lost in his own world and was blissfully oblivious to the others who were in the room.

"Approve of your mate, or the fact that he is apparently determined to purchase every book within a five-hundred-mile radius?" he asked, moving to her when she gestured to a spot on the sofa next to her.

"You are wyvern," she said in the same airy, slightly breathless voice that Drake remembered from his youth. "Of course you would approve of all green dragons, even ones who are not related to you by blood, as Jakab is. Although that is not strictly true, since he is a mere ten generations from the First Dragon, and that means your connection to him is separated only by four generations. Come. Have some of the wine I brought you."

She patted the sofa again, and he sat, accepting a glass of dragon's blood, sipping appreciably. "You have outdone yourself, Grand-mère. This is exceptional. What vintage is it?"

"It is the wine my Cziriak laid down when you were born," she answered, taking a small sip of it before setting down the glass and eyeing him, a glint of humor in her eyes. Drake knew those eyes well; he saw them each morning in his shaving mirror. "Your father tried to take it in order to woo Catalina, but fortunately, your grandfather hid it well, and Toldi only found your brother's birth-year vintage, and that, as you know, is undrinkable."

"Vinegar," Drake said, nodding, having a vague memory of Kostya ranting about the fact that there was some sort of a blight affecting the grapes that were produced the year he was born. "The fact that my father was still trying to woo Mother even after I was born is odd. She has not mentioned it."

Grand-mère waved away the question. "It is not important, given Toldi's end. Both of them. How is Catalina?"

"Well, I believe. At least, I have heard nothing to the contrary. The last time we spoke, she was living in South Africa."

"Ah. Diamonds," Grand-mère said, nodding.

"She always did like shiny things," he agreed.

"Just like a pet magpie that I had when you were a youngling. Do you remember Patois? He was not a very pretty bird, but he was so clever at finding objects to satisfy his need for shiny things." She smiled and patted Drake on the knee. "You were very much like him at the time."

He stiffened, wondering if she was insulting him. The idea was ridiculous, and yet, here she was making a comparison between him, the wyvern of the sept, and a motley, one-winged, flea-infested bird who regularly stole anything that caught his eye. "I did not make a habit of stealing from kin," he informed her with much hauteur.

"Ah, *kincsem*, you are so quick to take offense." She smiled, the wrinkles around her eyes creasing as she patted him on one cheek. "I'd tell you that you are just like your father, but I fear you would take offense of that, as well."

"Mother claims I get my temper from her," he answered, relaxing against the back of the sofa. Of course Grand-mère wasn't insulting him; no one loved him more than she did, and even her criticisms were gently delivered. "Naturally, I do not allow such unwelcome emotions to take hold of me."

"It is said that a wise man can control his emotions, but I've never found that to be at all practical," she observed, moving to adjust a pillow behind her. Drake rose to fetch a larger one, and assisted making her comfortable before retaking his seat. "Now, you will tell me what is bothering you so that I might return to Paris with an easy heart."

He was silent for a few minutes, considering her question. It was one he'd dealt with many times before, but evidently, she had once again returned to the subject of his love life, or lack thereof.

Part of him wanted to answer, to seek advice on a problem he couldn't speak of to anyone else, but he was well aware of the mantle of wyvernhood that clamped down upon him. He was a wyvern, and wyverns did not show weakness. "I must be a poor host if you believe I am troubled when I've been nothing but delighted to see you again."

"Drake," she said, shaking her head, but her eyes danced with amusement. "Do you think I am so unlearned that I cannot tell a dragon beset by worries, and one whose heart is carefree?"

"It's not a question of being unlearned," he said quickly, the emotional war within causing him to speak with more emphasis than was strictly called for. "I am a wyvern. Obviously, the cares of the sept fall upon my shoulders. If I seem less joyful than I was in the previous century, it is because I have heavier responsibilities settled on me."

"Now, that is an untruth. No, do not flare up at me," she said, lifting a hand to stop him even though he had done nothing more than give her a long look. "I am not insulting you, the most beloved of all my grandchildren."

"Kostya told me you say the same thing of him," he said, wiggling his shoulders to loosen them.

She laughed aloud, and surprised him by winking. "Your brother was always one to carry tales to you. It amazes me that he is the older, since he acts … but no. We are not here to discuss Kostya. Stop looking at me like I have piddled on your favorite cushion, *kincsem*. It is right and proper for you to wrap the dignity of your position around you, but haughtiness is unbecoming in a wyvern."

"The kin look to me for protection—" Drake started to protest, feeling momentarily adrift.

"They look to you for guidance. Respect. Love," she said, her gaze still a brilliant emerald, but the humor in it was replaced by a warning expression. "You were born to be wyvern, Drake. Yes, as was Kostya so born to be wyvern of the black sept, but you—you are special. You might not be a reeve as I am, but your bloodline is indisputable. You would not have been accepted by the green sept if it were otherwise."

Drake stood and moved to the window, twitching back a curtain to glance outside at the busy London street. "The sept is the only thing I'm concerned with, not the perceived value of my ancestry."

"It will have an impact when you find a mate," she continued, surprising him.

He turned back to face her, his sense of wariness fading. This was a familiar discussion. "You do not approve of my woman?"

"Which one?" she asked, a gentle smile curving her lips. "The mortal who graced your bed last night? The one whom you took to the opera the day before? Or the three who were disporting with you in the pool two nights past?"

He took an involuntary step back.

"Oh, yes," she said, taking another sip of wine, her eyes downright sparkling with merriment. "I know of your escapades. Your brother stopped by to visit me, and later went to find you. He says he left immediately, but not before he saw you were engaged in what was an extremely spirited aquatic session of sexual congress. Ah, I see by your expression that you remember the time many years ago when we had a talk about a mate. You were troubled then, and you are more so now. This concerns me."

Drake sent another quick glance at Jakab, but the latter was now seated on the floor, bent over a book the size of a bulldog. Drake cherished all members of his sept, but he had a fondness for the scholar who had kept his grandmother from becoming lonely. "I've made myself clear on the subject of females, mortal and drag-onkin. As for troubles, I have none other than keeping Chuan Ren from destroying as many green dragons as she can."

He stopped, badly wanting reassurance, but unwilling for her to know the truth.

And yet … there was literally no one else he trusted more. His mother would be sympathetic, but she'd been born mortal, and despite her belief she was a source of dragon lore, her grasp on that subject was less than complete. He'd get no answers from her.

Kostya would not do at all. Likewise any of his sept, or even those dragons whom he considered friends.

There was no one but Grand-mère to ask. His choice was to bare his soul to her or keep silent about it for the balance of his life.

"Yes?" Grand-mère asked, sipping at her wine, just as if she'd read his mind.

He shot a suspicious glance at her, but her face was placid and filled with mild curiosity.

"I … there is something I would ask you," he said slowly, fighting the need to keep his secret shame hidden, tired of the doubt.

Wyverns never doubted. Not about themselves, anyway.

Grand-mère gave him an encouraging smile.

"It is … over the past two hundred years, I've found it … there is difficulty …" He stopped, unwilling to put into words the true depths of his fear.

She said nothing, just raised her eyebrows in question, and waited for him to continue.

He drained his wineglass and, with a muttered oath, said quickly, "I have difficulty shifting form."

"Ah?" She thought for a moment, then nodded. "That is what is troubling you? My Drake, my *kincsem*, that is a normal situation."

"It is?" He frowned, relieved but at the same time hesitant. "Kostya can shift at the merest wish. My guards can do the same. I do not know of any other dragon who has problems shifting to dragon form when it is so desired."

"I cannot," she answered, surprising him. "Like you, I was born of a black dragon father, but he placed me with my mother's family because I was a reeve. Those of us who were born to one sept but accepted by another have found that our ability to show our primal selves is hindered."

"I used to be able to shift," he admitted softly, not wishing for Jakab to hear, even though Drake doubted he was listening. "But I have not done so recently."

"When was the last time?" she asked.

"About 1680."

"You were a youngling then, under a hundred." She gave a shrug. "As you grew into your green dragon self and embraced what it was to be a dragon—and a wyvern's heir—your ability to shift subsided to allow the growth of more important facets of your being. It is the way of things with those kin who are special."

"I don't like it," he said, forcing his fingers to relax when he wanted nothing more than to shout at the unfairness of it all.

Wyverns did not shout about unfairness.

"That is understandable, but if it is that which has kept you from thinking you will find a mate, then I can assure you that the opposite is true. As we have proof," she said, nodding toward Jakab.

Drake considered this new information. "He must be an extraordinary dragon, indeed, if he is willing to overlook our shared ... trait."

She smiled at her mate. "He is. As you are, and as will be your mate when you find her."

"I don't think that will happen," he countered, shaking his head.

"Then I will greatly enjoy saying 'I told you so' later, when you find her. Do not look so crestfallen, my Drake. Our trait, as you called it, is simply the price we pay to be ourselves, and I would not have you change to be what you believe others want," Grand-mère answered, then took his face in her hands, studying him for a minute before adding, "There is much of Cziriak's compassion in you, but you have more intelligence."

She must have noted his startled expression, because she laughed when he sputtered a protest.

"You need not defend your grandsire's honor, Drake. He was many things, but I knew full well he was not the brightest of dragons. Your father was the opposite—he had all the cunning his father lacked, and none of his compassion. You, on the other hand, have been graced with little of your father's nature, for which we are all thankful. Instead, you are filled with compassion tempered with intuition, and I have no doubt at all that you will be an extremely capable wyvern if you let go of doubt, and trust yourself."

"It is not myself I doubt, but the sanity of others," he grumbled, but a tension inside him eased somewhat.

"With that, I cannot help," she said, patting him on the leg before getting to her feet. He'd noticed she was starting to show signs of age, something that eluded most dragons until they could count their lifetime in four digits. She straightened up, adding, "And now I must return home so that I may attend the ladies' group I joined to prepare."

"Prepare for what?" he asked, rising and following after her. "The situation with Belgium? I doubt it will come to much. The mortals may not be wise, but they are not going to throw away their lives on pride and egotism."

Grand-mère tapped Jakab on his shoulder, making him start before immediately getting to his feet. "You think not? You've seen many wars over the last four hundred years. Do you not see the signs now of more fighting?"

Drake was mildly annoyed with himself. He'd been so preoccupied with ensuring the safety of the green dragons, he hadn't paid much attention to the death of an archduke. "What do you and the mortals do at this group?"

"Dreary things, no doubt," she said, taking his arm as they strolled toward the front door, Jakab instructing one of the servants on how to properly pack up the boxes of his newly acquired books. "There will be the knitting of socks and balaclavas, gathering stores and medical supplies—that reminds me, you might warn any of the sept who have medical experience to be available should they be needed—fundraising and all the so-very-tedious things that women do."

"If it is unpleasant to you, then simply do not involve yourself. The mortals will do as they do without our aid," he pointed out.

"Ah, but could I do what I do?" She smiled when they stopped on the pavement next to a gleaming motorcar. Drake had given it to his grand-mère on her last birthday, an act that resulted in him obtaining three of the vehicles for himself. "That is to say, could I live with myself? The answer is no. I must help mortals, just as I've always done in times of their need. Have no fear for us, *kincsem*—Jakab and I will be tucked away quite safely in Paris, far away from all the goings-on in Austria and Hungary. It eases my mind to know that you and Kostya are in England, as well."

Drake didn't like the idea that his beloved grand-mère was working so hard for mortals who brought their own doom upon themselves, but accepted that now was not the time to reason with her.

He kissed her good-bye, watching as the car—now laden with crates of books—drove off, telling himself she would be fine, and he did not need to shut her away in a safehold to keep the ills of the world from her.

THREE

29 March 1918

Grand-mère is gone, as is Jakab, and two mortal members of their staff. If I could locate the one who ordered the bombing ... but that is folly. I wish to fight, to rage against the circumstance, to beat to death everything that led to Grand-mère being where she was at that moment in time. If the mortals hadn't warred, she wouldn't have died. It is their fault she spent the last four years trying to aid them. It is her blood that stains the hands of the mortal race.

Drake fought the urge to roar his fury to the world, knowing that it was grief that drove the anger at the senseless loss of so many innocents.

He had never much worried over mortals as his grandam had, but even he was appalled by the news of a bombing in Paris that had led to not just the death of his grandmother and her mate, but that of a hundred innocent mortals.

His shoulders bowed as the grief once again washed over him, threatening to consume him. He struggled for a few minutes to get his emotions under control, then lifted his pen again.

I must think of the sept. The green dragons will survive this loss just as we survive all others ... together.

I will not forget, however. I will never forget.

18 June 1966

Roughly fifty years have passed since I've seen this journal. I found it in a crate of books I brought to France. I really must stick to a schedule to write, since a record of the green sept will be of interest to all.

"What would it take to hire you?"

Drake set down his pen and closed the stained, somewhat battered leather journal, and accepted a glass offered to him by Albert Camus, the Venediger who more or less ruled over the European Otherworld. His gaze shifted down the bar of G&T, absently noting the number of people, beings, and spirits who were currently enjoying their time in what was indisputably Paris's premiere club for immortal beings.

"That would depend on what you wanted me to do," he answered at last, taking a sip of dragon's blood. Behind him, he felt the presence of his two elite guards, Pal and István, and, judging by the stifled squawk and the scrape of barstool on the stone floor, suspected they moved in to squeeze out the couple of people who had been sitting near him. Although he didn't really need the protection the two men offered, it was a tradition that all wyverns honored, and he wouldn't dream of going against it.

Besides, it had been decades since he could bear the memories that followed his return to Paris, and he was happy to let all there know that the two redheaded green dragons from his native Hungary had his favor.

"Everyone knows the green dragons are master thieves," Albert said, nodding when one of the servers came up to gain approval for a transaction. "And it is said that the most talented of all is their wyvern."

"You wish for me to acquire something?" Drake asked, his interest piqued. "What is it? Something to do with G&T, or something for your personal collection?"

"The latter … of a sort." Albert matched the intensity of Drake's gaze. "It is a historical artifact."

"Ah." Drake's pulse quickened. Historical items were often made of precious metals, like gold.

"I thought that would interest you," Albert said with a small smile. "I'm afraid I have no idea how to obtain the artifact. That will be part of the challenge."

"I have been thinking of late that I would benefit from joining the international police force—Interpol—since they always seem to be involved whenever objects of great wealth go missing," Drake said slowly, his mind racing from thought to thought. Why would the Venediger seek a historical artifact? So far as Drake knew, Albert had a collection of dueling weapons, and those were a far cry from the items Drake desired. "This could be the push I need to investigate the requirements for a high-level position within."

"Why Interpol?" Albert asked with eyes that were suddenly shuttered.

"They have an entire roomful of files detailing information about the world's most valuable objects," Drake answered succinctly. "Naturally, that is something I very much wish to see."

"Naturally," the Venediger said, obviously relaxing. He went so far as to allow a second slight smile to flit across his lips. "How you acquire the object is not the issue. I desire it, and I'm willing to pay you for it."

Drake leaned against the long, smooth brass and mahogany bar. "What is the object?"

"A chalice," Albert answered after a quick glance around him. Pal and István were doing much to keep bystanders from getting within range of earshot, Drake was pleased to note. "One crafted roughly six hundred years ago. There is a rumor it was given to a mage who passed it over into control of the L'au-dela, and is currently housed in the Committee's vault at Suffrage House here in Paris. I would like to know if that's true, the status of ownership, and whether you would be able to acquire it on my behalf."

Drake's eyes had widened at the last couple of sentences. Although he had no false modesty about his particular set of skills, he had never been able to get into the famed L'au-dela vault, rumored to be a bastion of security. It was a description he reluctantly agreed with after trying to break in four different times over two hundred years.

Still, the thought was tantalizing. "It is said the vault is impregnable," he said, running his fingers around the rim of his wineglass. "One that many have tried to breach, but all failed."

"Those who tried were not you," Albert said with a smoothness that irritated Drake.

He ignored the compliment, not wanting to admit his previous failures. "And in return, you offer … ?"

Albert's lips thinned. "I don't suppose money would be acceptable?"

Drake sipped his wine, saying nothing.

"As I thought," Albert said on a sigh. "Very well. I believe you have a fondness for Vermeer, yes? I happen to have recently added to my nascent art collection a charming, heretofore uncatalogued Vermeer. Three experts have verified its veracity. I'd be happy to offer that in exchange for the chalice."

Drake's interest skyrocketed with each word. That Albert was offering something like an unknown Vermeer hinted the chalice was more valuable than he'd thought. He wondered if it was made of gold; if so, then he would most definitely work to locate it … but it would remain with him, not the Venediger.

"That would be agreeable, dependent upon my own expert evaluating the painting," he answered, not overly bothered by lack of morals when it came to gold objects.

"This is an illustration of the chalice. It was made by an alchemist mage some six hundred years ago. It is called the Voce di Lucifer." Albert slid over a photocopy of an old line drawing, clearly from an antique grimoire. Drake didn't fail to notice that although Albert's voice was that of a man talking about something unimportant, his eyes—half-lidded as they were—could not conceal a gleam of excitement.

"Voice of Lucifer?" Drake asked, his brows pulling together as he racked his memory for such an object. He drew a blank. "That is an odd name for an item created by a mage."

"Alchemist mage," Albert corrected, speaking softly to the bartender when the latter murmured a question relating to a missing shipment of beverages. He turned back to Drake with a face carefully devoid of anything but the mildest expression of interest. "What do you think? Are you up to the challenge?"

Drake knew full well the Venediger chose his words specifically to prick his sense of pride, but he dismissed that, just as he did the morality of taking for himself something he was being paid to retrieve for another.

It had been well over eighty years since he last had a go at the vault. It was time to finally crack that particular nut. He took a sip of the wine, enjoying the heat of it on his tongue, and finally dipped his head in accord. "It is a challenge, indeed, but not one that should be beyond the scope of the green dragons."

They discussed for a few more minutes the exact terms of the agreement, and by the time Drake left, he was already plotting how to get into the Committee's headquarters, where the vault was located.

FOUR

28 February 1967

"Are you sure this is going to work? It seems some-what—I don't want to say naive, but perhaps reckless?—to base your plan to storm Western Europe's most secure storage on a movie premise." The Guardian named Patrice stood with Drake outside Suffrage House, eyeing its imposing white stone facade. Drake was under no illusion that the plan that had finally formed was not incredibly bizarre, but given the extensive precautions the Committee had taken over the last eight months after each of his attempts, he had little choice. It was this or go completely back to the drawing board.

"It will work so long as you can break all the wards and prohibitions," he answered, checking his watch. They had two minutes before a handful of green dragons would start a distraction at the back entrance. "Do you have the demons you will need?"

"Not on me, but yes, they are ready for summoning." The Guardian gave him an odd look. "I don't know how you're going to get through the lock; the peek I had at it last week was beyond daunting."

"That reminds me, I must also reclaim the grimoire you used to get access to the vault," Drake murmured to himself before addressing her statement. "Do not worry about the lock. It will yield to Mattio. He has trained for the last three hundred years, and there is no lock he cannot best."

"Mm-hmm," Patrice answered, but didn't look convinced.

The slight explosion that Drake was expecting sounded then, causing him to settle into the glamour that changed his (very well-known) appearance. Taking Patrice's arm, he escorted her into Suffrage House.

It took little time to find the cleaners' closet on the basement floor that his sept members had found on one of many previous sweeps of the building—sweeps that were usually cut short as soon as the Watch realized who they were. With only a fast glance at the stairs that led down to the subbasement where the vault was located, he joined Patrice in the small, musty closet, carefully shutting the door in a way that left him able to open it from the inside.

"What now?" she asked him when he made himself comfortable on the floor while she perched on a up-turned bucket.

"We wait for the offices to shut, and the building to go into its night routine," he answered.

"You know, I saw that Audrey Hepburn movie, too," Patrice said after a few minutes of silence, which Drake spent listening intently. "It was fun, but not very likely. Although I have to admit, the security people don't seem to have noticed us entering. How many others have you stashed away throughout the building?"

"Several. They will have no direct impact on opening the vault, however."

"Protection?" she asked.

He nodded, and resumed his stance of intense listening; his nerves jangled, and his dragon fire was unusually high.

Four hours and twenty minutes later, just when Drake had stood to relieve his cramped muscles, his watch made a tinny pinging sound.

"Hrm?" Beside him, Patrice jerked from where she'd slumped while dozing. "Is it time?"

"Yes," Drake said, and, emerging from the closet, glanced down the empty hallway, dimly lit by a screened light.

They hurried toward the door that led downward, their footsteps hushed, but echoing nonetheless. Drake was aware of his kin around him, hidden in various spots throughout the interior of Suffrage House; even with that reassurance, his breath was quick, and his heart beat loudly in his ears.

"I guess it's showtime," Patrice said once they arrived in front of the heavy steel vault door.

Pal, István, and Mattio emerged from the far hallway at a run, but after a moment's alarm, Drake relaxed. Their expressions were content, not worried.

Patrice summoned a demon, one in the form of a bored female in a large blond hairstyle that Drake recalled was referred to as a beehive. The demon chewed gum loudly as it argued with Patrice, but in the end, broke the prohibitions on the door while Patrice tackled the wards.

"The security system?" Drake asked Pal.

"Down," he answered with a grin.

Patrice glanced over, having finished with the wards. "You disabled it? I thought the wires were protected by a housing that couldn't be cut."

"Cut? No. Melted, yes," István said with grim satisfaction.

"Did you use some sort of a torch? I didn't think such things got hot enough to affect the alarm housing," she said, her gaze on the demon as it broke the last prohibition.

"Dragon fire can do much that mortal torches can't," István said with dignity. Drake, who was waiting, moved forward the instant the last prohibition melted into nothing, beckoning at Mattio.

"Ah. Yes. I see." The dragon, who wore the same mildly befuddled expression as had his grand-mère's mate, studied the lock. He was an elder, a good seven hundred years older than Drake, one who lived the life of a solitary scholar.

The fact that he was the best safe cracker in all the L'au-dela was not known to anyone outside the sept, and both Mattio and Drake were quite happy keeping it that way.

It took the dragon fifteen minutes before he managed to work his way through the many layers of mechanism, but at last the door was open.

"I'll check it out first," Drake said as he gestured at his men to remain behind. If there was a trap inside the vault, or something that posed a threat, he preferred to keep his kin safe.

Insert the vault, the air was slightly warm and resonant with the scent of old books, incense, and ... he tipped his head back and breathed deeply.

Gold. There was gold here.

His blood lit with dragon fire as he moved silently into the antechamber, aware of air circulating around him, a faint hum from overhead fluorescent lights, and the soft tapping of something wooden.

He strode past rows of metal cases, each labeled with the contents, everything from grimoires to diaries, a variety of objects that had been deemed by the Committee as too dangerous to be available to the mortal and immortal worlds, and even a few silver-chased cases bearing cursed items. Drake quickly scanned the labels of all the cases, but none were what he was looking for.

Carefully, he proceeded through the door to the next room, and came to a halt at the sight of a man—no, not a man, a spirit—who was surrounded by imps in tiny elaborate Edwardian dresses, complete with large hats and parasols.

"—if I've told you once, I've told you a hundred times that this scene is all about elegance. You need to get in that headspace! Let's go over it again—you are at Ascot with all the other nobility. You are rich and above such things as being excited at horse races. You stroll—STROLL—around with slow, languid movements. Only Eliza leaps around when the horses pass by. Do you hear? Only Eliza! Now, let us try it again. Places! Wait—where is Eliza?"

Drake blinked once to make sure he hadn't suddenly started hallucinating. The spirit jumped to his feet and stormed around calling for Eliza before he noticed Drake in the door.

"We're closed," the spirit told him.

"Indeed. And you are … ?"

"Misha." The spirit considered him sourly. "You're a dragon."

"I am Drake Vireo, wyvern of the green dragons," he said with a bow.

Misha made a tsking sound in the back of his throat. "Here to be a bother, no doubt. Well, you can go away until the vault is open tomorrow morning. As you see, I have much to do, far too much for the sanity of one man. We have only three weeks before we're due to be televised on Cavalcade of the Otherworld TV show, and the imps simply refuse to understand how this scene works. It's as much as a spirit can stand, let me tell you. No, no, do not run to the railing to see the horses … stroll. You know how to stroll, don't you?"

Drake considered his options, decided that he didn't have the time or inclination to find out why a vault keeper was evidently putting on a production of My Fair Lady with Australian House Imps, and instead simply gathered his dragon fire into his hands before directing it at the spirit's head.

He caught a second of Misha's surprised expression before the latter succumbed to the immediate drastic drop in the energy needed to keep himself in corporeal mode, and disappeared into nothing.

The imps cheered, and scattered to a series of what looked like elaborate dollhouses lined up against the far wall.

It took less than a minute to locate the lockbox containing the chalice. A few minutes of bathing the box in his fire had it crumbling into nothing, leaving inside a blackened, smoking silver box.

Drake extracted from it a golden goblet encrusted in emeralds. The scent of the gold damned near drove him to madness, but he tucked it away in the charred box and left the vault.

"The Voce di Lucifer," he said two hours later when he, with Pal and István at his side, gently placed the chalice onto a shelf in his personal vault beneath his Paris house. It wasn't as secure as his lair, but that was back in Hungary, and he very much wanted to enjoy his new acquisition for a while before it had to be hidden away. "The Venediger has excellent taste in chalices."

"Very nice," István said, rubbing his nose. Drake knew just how he felt. The scent of the gold went straight to his head and left him struggling to control base emotions.

"Pretty. It has dragons on it, did you see?" Pal asked, leaning forward to study it. He, too, rubbed his nose. "Bah. I can't get that close to it without … well …"

"I'm going to find Suzanne," István announced, and, turning on his heel, marched out of the room in order to find his mate, who acted as cook for Drake's household.

Pal laughed, then grimaced when he tried to walk. "I don't often wish to be tied down to a woman, since I must go wherever you travel, but this is one of the times when I dearly wish I had someone upon whom I could slake this lust."

Drake ignored the erection that resulted from the nearness of the chalice. "Have you heard of the Tools of Bael?" he asked Pal, adjusting a subdued spotlight so that it just glanced off the artifact.

"No. Should I have?" Pal asked, moving toward the door.

Drake was silent for a minute before he turned and followed Pal out, making sure to set all the alarms and locks on the door. "It seems to be a well-kept secret, if the trouble I had digging out information was anything to judge by. There are three objects, one the chalice I acquired, one a lodestone chased in gold, and the third an aquamanile."

Pal slid him a look as they climbed the stairs to the main floor. "If it's such a big secret, then no one will notice if the other two pieces of the set disappear."

Drake allowed himself a small, satisfied smile. The need to possess the three pieces had moved to the top of his interest list. "That is exactly how I feel. The trouble is finding them. My preliminary research indicates that the Anima di Lucifer is held privately in the States, while the Occhio was last seen in Italy about thirty years ago."

"It's too bad the Interpol people didn't accept you," Pal said, his gaze amused as Drake strode to his library without comment. The subject of his repeated attempts to get into the organization that held on to so many tantalizing bits of information still rankled.

He made a mental oath he would get into the organization, or die trying.

14 July 2004
Once again, I have stumbled across this journal. It has a curious way of disappearing and reappearing at odd moments, but perhaps that is due to my lack of interest in recording the goings-on of the green dragons. I would throw it out altogether, but it was Grand-mère's wish that I keep a journal, and so I shall.

The phone rang just as he was mulling over what news to record in the journal.

"Drakeling! You are avoiding your dearest mama! I will not have this! I did not go through the many hours, the many, many days, of the most horrendous torture while the midwives ripped you from my womb only for you to turn your back upon me! You hate me! You have turned down the path of your so-deranged father, and you hate me! Admit it to me, the one who almost died giving you life."

Upon hearing the sultry, Spanish-accented voice of his mother, doña Catalina de Elférez, Drake heaved a mental sigh, and damned the fact that he'd recently given her the number of his mobile phone.

Life was so much easier in the days when she had to be on the same continent to speak to him.

"I will not honor the statement regarding hating you, because we both know it is rubbish. As for your other claim, the last thing I could do is avoid you, Mother," he answered in what he'd come to think of as his Catalina tone. Only she could both drive him to distraction and amuse him. He suspected that it was her Latin blood in him that led to his secret enjoyment of her dramatic scenes. "For one, you pop up too regularly for me to even begin avoiding you, and for another, there is no other woman alive who can enrage me one moment and make me laugh the next."

"You should be glad there is no one such like me," Catalina answered without a care toward proper grammar. "For if there were, you would be in love with her instantly."

"I don't know about that," he said slowly, his mind filling with horror at the idea of falling for a woman who both annoyed and intrigued him. "It's a moot point, since I will never take a mate. What is it you want? I don't wish to be brusque, but I have an appointment I cannot miss."

"Is it not said that all men desire their mothers for mates?" Catalina continued, ignoring his question just as he knew she would. "I, myself, longed for a man as good as my so beloved papa. He was the handsomest, the most courtly of men. All the women loved him. Even some of the men, but that was not spoken of at that time. But my papa, how full of joy he was. Before Toldi killed him, naturally. Afterward, he held a grudge toward us, and insisted on retreating into the spirit world with Mama. I will never forgive Toldi for not only killing my entire family but driving them all into the spirit realm simply so they could avoid him. It was all so unfortunate. You bear some of my saint-ed father's appearance, thank the Virgin, and not that of your demented father, although poor Kostya sadly favors him. It is his nose, I think. It is so very thin and straight, like the edge of the razor. Have you heard from him?"

"Father?" Drake asked, both startled by the idea and confused by his mother's unorthodox use of pronouns. "Did you have him resurrected again? I thought the last time—"

Catalina gave a ladylike snort of disgust. "No, no, why would I do such a thing? The only reason I had him brought back before was to see if death had im-proved him at all. It did not."

"No, it didn't," Drake agreed, thinking of the report of Toldi's resurrection he'd heard from Kostya a few hundred years earlier. "Despite that, I still feel it was inappropriate to have his scrotum made into jewelry after you killed him a second time."

"Madre de Dios, did you think I was not due ugly earrings after what I put up from that maniac?"

Drake interrupted what he was sure was going to be a lengthy—and familiar—tirade about what his mother had (admittedly) suffered when his father had claimed her as his mate. "I must leave, Mother. What is it you need?"

"You speak to me in such a manner? Me, who lay on the altar of childbirth for days on end—"

"The car is waiting for me. You have one minute, and then I must hang up," he said, ignoring the fact that he was on a mobile phone, and not the landline.

"I will not have this—"

"Forty-five seconds," he said, fighting his dragon fire, which was fairly burning along his blood, making him feel itchy with anticipation.

The Anima di Lucifer had been found. It had arrived in Paris that very day, and he knew to whom it had been delivered.

"I did not raise you to speak in such a manner!" Catalina snapped. Drake bit back the urge to laughingly remind her she hadn't raised him at all, since he'd been sent to live with his grand-mère when he was barely walking. "But since you are the son of my heart, the blood of my blood, I shall give way to you as I always do."

He did laugh at that, but managed to cover up the mouthpiece before she could hear. "I appreciate that."

"It is your brother. Have you heard from him? He has not contacted me for … oh, it must be sixty years? Seventy? When was it that all the Nazis ran to South America?"

"Mid-1940s," he answered, nodding when István opened the door and tipped his head toward the front door. "And no, I have not heard from him, but it was his decision to go underground to find any remaining black dragons before he returned to the weyr."

"That is odd, though, is it not?" Catalina said with a click of her tongue. "This silence?"

"Not given the current makeup of the weyr. You know full well how Kostya is about the silver dragons—he will cause endless trouble about them when he does surface, and Gabriel will respond with little patience. Thus, I am content for Kostya to remain out of sight of other dragons. And now I must go, Mother."

"I do not like this silence. It is not like him—"

Drake clicked off the call, and spent the ride to the aquamanile's owner in contemplation of how he would present the Anima once he had it.

"What will you tell the Venediger when you refuse to give him the aquamanile?" Pal asked when they were paused at a light. "He's not going to be happy with us. He's still bitter about the loss of the chalice."

"The green dragons have survived worse than an unhappy Venediger," he said, glancing up at the large building that obviously housed several high-end apartments. He waved back both guards. "And since he believed me when I said I was unable to break into the L'au-dela vault forty years ago, all is well. No, I will do this on my own, in case Albert was suspicious and has set some sort of a trap for us. Return for me no later than thirty minutes."

He felt the prickle of awareness as soon as he entered the building. It was oddly silent, and he thought once or twice that he caught a faint scent of a dark being, most likely a demon.

But it was when he entered a sunny sitting room filled with embroidered antique furniture that he stopped, as the sense of foreboding, scent of demon, and general aura of something being not right coalesced.

A body of a middle-aged woman hung by hands tied behind her back. That she was dead was clear, which meant that someone had taken issue to her owning the aquamanile.

"Peste," he swore, and wondered who would kill a mortal with such obvious pointers to the Otherworld. Albert wouldn't be so stupid, especially since he thought Drake was acquiring the artifact for him.

With an annoyed tsk, he quickly searched the rooms of the apartment but found no sign of life. He called the mortal police, figuring he had about ten minutes before they'd arrive. It wasn't until three minutes later when he returned from checking a service balcony that he heard noises indicating someone else was in the apartment.

"The Anima," he murmured, and hurried to the sitting room, there to see a woman with wildly curly hair lean in as if she was going to touch the dead woman. "No!" he told her, leaping forward when she made an odd squawk and fell toward the body.

He managed to get her before she breached the circle of salt on the carpet, jerking her back, the scent of her suddenly filling his nose.

His body reacted in a way that made him think of a time a few centuries before when he'd touched the coil of a primitive battery, the hairs on his arms standing on end with the woman's nearness.

She spoke in an atrocious version of French, her accent belying her origins.

"American?" he asked, trying to catch her scent. It was a heady mixture of light floral notes tinged with an earthier base of sun-warmed fields, and to his immense confusion, it fired both his libido and his interest in the woman. He studied her, more than a little surprised to find she was a Guardian. He'd assumed by the clumsy way she'd almost thrown herself on the dead woman that she was mortal.

"Yes." She glanced around, obviously overwhelmed. He wondered if she had something to do with the death, not being particularly concerned if she was. It was nothing to do with him ... although he wouldn't have been averse to inviting her to his bed. There was something about her, something in her hazel eyes, that stirred his interest.

"I did not kill her," he reassured the woman when she suddenly realized the circumstance in which she found herself. Fear coursed through her, driving his dragon fire through his veins.

What was this madness? No mortal woman had ever stirred his fire, and precious few dragon females. For him to be reacting this way now ...

She made a face, and he worried she was going to be sick at the sight of the dead woman.

On the whole, he thought as he kept her talking just to see what she would say, it was doubtful that she'd killed the mortal.

That said, it was probably wiser for him to take the aquamanile and leave the strangely intriguing Guardian. He distracted her with a few questions about the circle of ash, trying to come to a decision.

His mind told him to get the Anima di Lucifer and wash his hands of the woman, but the dragon part of him demanded that he investigate the strange reaction she stirred within him.

"What does fear smell like, exactly?" the woman asked in answer to one of his statements.

An image flashed in his mind, that of her racing through a forest, her hair streaming behind her as she dodged around trees and leaped over small shrubs, all the while he followed, tracking her by the scent of fear left on the air. "Sexy," he said, willing his body to cease its attempt to woo her.

There would be time enough for that later. He was mildly startled by that thought, but couldn't pay attention to it while he had to deal with the situation before him.

"What?" the woman asked, and he answered something—just what escaped him, for the moment he

leaned forward to make a point by staring straight
into her eyes, he felt himself on the edge of a precipice,
about to fall into the haze of arousal and intrigue that
seemed to surround her.

It took an effort, but at last he managed to distract
her by asking her questions about who had drawn the
circle, and why, and when it became clear she was too
suspicious, he pulled out the identity card he'd kept after he'd been removed from Interpol.

He smiled to himself. He'd lasted six months before
they finally discovered that he was accessing databases
far above his clearance level.

"Wait a minute! I didn't just fall off the stupid wagon. I want to see that up close," the woman demanded
when he tucked away his wallet.

"If the circle is closed, how did the demon escape?"
he asked her in a blatant attempt to distract.

It worked. He spent the next few minutes indulging in a mental argument about whether he should just
leave, or if further investigation into the woman was
warranted.

She continued to argue with him, and it wasn't until
she told him her name—Aisling Grey—and that she
was a courier, that he realized it was she and not the
dead woman who had the Anima.

He breathed in deeply again, this time catching the
faintest hint of something other than her fascinating
scent. "Gold," he told her when she insisted her statue
was just ordinary metal. "The statue is of gold."

The combination of the Guardian and the scent of
the gold left him on the edge of arousal. Aisling made
a fuss about him not acting like a policeman, but he
couldn't remain focused on his cover story. Not when
he found himself caught in twin demands of possess-

ing the aquamanile ... and the woman. He wasn't the least bit startled by the realization that he wanted her in a sexual way—it seemed perfectly natural given the fact that her presence seemed to bind him to her with a thousand silken ropes made up of the most exquisite anticipation.

What was out of the ordinary was the way something inside him seemed to thrum when she drew near.

Wyverns didn't thrum, especially at mortals.

Except Aisling proved that one wyvern, at least, was vulnerable to the effect of her presence.

"Let me go!" Aisling demanded when he drew her to him, unable to keep from running his hands along her hips and back, and breathing in deeply of her scent so as to commit it to memory. His body was hot and hard with need, but he kept himself in check as he brushed a strand of her wild, curly hair back from her cheek, and then, unable to resist, leaned in to taste her lips.

She was as sweet as honey, and as heady as dragon's blood.

He stole the aquamanile while she stood with her mouth slightly parted, and her eyes soft with passion.

"What? Hey! You can't kiss me!" Her voice followed as he bolted out of the apartment, the mortal police sirens warning they had arrived. He left by a door leading out to a back alley, the echo of her words trailing after him.

"Stop! That's mine!"

"Not any longer," Drake said, mingled satisfaction and sexual frustration leaving him feeling strangely empty.

Ten minutes later, he rode in the back seat of the car, the case bearing the Anima on his knees, his gaze sightlessly watching as the streets of Paris passed by.

Just who was the Guardian who denied her birthright? Why did she appear so clueless about her profession and the Otherworld, and yet at the same time oddly knowledgeable about other things? Was she deceiving him for some purpose, or was she simply as naive as she appeared?

He had a feeling he'd be seeing her soon, if for no other reason than he suspected she'd go after him for the loss of the aquamanile.

"Good," he said, smiling at nothing. He very much looked forward to their next meeting, ignoring the fact that he hadn't been so captivated by a female in a long time. "We shall see how hard you try to recover what you lost, Guardian."

"Eh?" Pal asked from the front seat, glancing over his shoulder to Drake.

"Nothing. Let us go straight home. I wish to put the Anima with the Voce di Lucifer."

"The Venediger isn't going to be happy," Pal pointed out again.

"It is of no matter," Drake answered, his mind on the Guardian named Aisling. He wished he could pinpoint what it was about her that had such a profound effect on him, but he'd never been one for too much introspection. It was one reason why he continually forgot about the journal he'd been determined to keep.

Aisling Grey. It was an unusual name for an unusual woman. He wondered how she'd react when she found out he was a dragon, and smiled again.

He couldn't help but look forward to that discovery.

FIVE

15 July 2004

I met a Guardian yesterday. She is an interesting contradiction of perceptive and ignorant, or at least that's the impression I gained. I believe I will—

"Drake, the Venediger has asked to see you. I told him you were busy, but he insists." István stood next to where Drake sat in his favorite booth tucked away in the back of G&T, attempting once again to make some notes in his rediscovered journal.

He looked up, his brows pulled together. "I've already explained to him that I did not find the aquamanile at the mortal's house. There is nothing more to discuss."

István gave a one-shoulder shrug. "I'm passing along the request." The emphasis on the last word was impossible to ignore.

Drake thought of doing just that, but after a moment's consideration of how difficult the Venediger could make his time in Paris, he tucked away the journal and rose, moving to the bar where Albert stood in his usual spot at the end.

"There is a rumor," Albert said before he could even offer a greeting, "put about by the police that a mortal has lodged a charge stating you have stolen a valuable artifact while she was at Madame Deauxville's house."

Drake arranged his expression to display surprise. "How curious. What is the artifact I am supposed to have stolen?"

Albert's eyes were steady on his, and Drake was aware that although he had no great affection for the Venediger, he had to respect the amount of power the latter all but exuded. "I hoped you would tell me."

"I have nothing," Drake said, lifting his hands in a gesture of innocence. "Ah, I see. You believe I took the aquamanile that you hired me to locate. I would like to point out that I am not known for cheating others. In addition, I can't help but wonder why you'd believe that a mortal would have possession of such an incredibly valuable object. It's not as if it's something that has changed hands often, as I well know. It's one of the few things I was able to trace during my all-too-brief time with Interpol."

"Yes, yes, you told me that you'd traced it to the last world war, where it disappeared into Italy, and that it was only six months ago that it came to auction and was sold to an American collector. That does not explain the fact that some mortal is claiming you stole something valuable from her."

Drake pretended to think about the matter. "I did see a mortal woman at the house where I believe the aquamanile was being held, but she objected to me kissing her. No doubt she seeks some type of revenge by attempting to send the police after me. It does not concern me. If every woman I kissed tried to have me arrested, I'd never set foot out of jail."

"No, I see that," Albert said slowly. Disappointment flashed in his eyes for a few seconds before his face donned his usual placid expression. "Your reputation being what it is when it comes to mortal women ... yes. Very well, I will dismiss my concern about the mortal, and instead repeat my request that you double your efforts to find the Anima."

Drake bowed his head in acknowledgment and murmured, "I will do everything within my power to locate the two remaining Tools of Bael."

Before Albert could answer, he was summoned to take a call in one of the back offices, and Drake was left at the bar counter, Pal and István next to him.

"I believe we will have no further problems about the American woman," Drake told his men in a volume limited to their ears. "Albert is—"

"Well, if it isn't Puff the Magic Dragon."

Drake stiffened at the voice, then immediately felt his fire surge to life, demanding he give in to his dragon nature and claim the woman who had haunted his dreams the night before.

He turned around to find Aisling Grey, Guardian, stomping forward toward him, her antagonistic expression both amusing him and warning that she had more of a temper than he'd originally thought.

"You have something of mine, Drake. I want it back. *Now*."

Behind him, Pal gave a little gasp. Drake knew just how his guard felt—he, himself, was more than a little astounded by the audacity of the Guardian.

"I had not expected to see you here," he managed to say, clamping down on the fire inside him that warned he needed an outlet to indulge in all the fantasies that had plagued his sleep the night before.

"I'm sure you didn't. I want my aquamanile back," she answered, and before he could do more than narrow his eyes on her, she poked him in the chest.

Poked him! In the chest! He was a wyvern! No one who wanted to see the sun rise the following morning poked a wyvern in the chest, and yet here was this woman, this mortal, who dared do just that. Not to mention the fact that she continued to berate him about taking the Anima. He dismissed the ridiculous notion that he'd return something he claimed, and instead told her he had almost fallen for her innocent act.

"It wasn't an act," she answered, lifting her chin, an action that both annoyed and delighted him. The fact that she had no idea who he was, or what respect was due him, was evident.

He would have to see to her education.

"Are you by any chance threatening me?" he asked when she continued to chastise him.

István and Pal kept sliding odd glances his way, but at a signal from Drake, they relaxed back into leaning on the bar and watching Aisling as she continued to argue.

"Only if you intend on making things hard," she answered, her chin lifting again.

Drake, on the whole, was a circumspect man, despite Kostya's propensity to walk in on him at awkward moments. He didn't believe in public displays of affection, he seldom raised his voice outside his own home, and he preferred to keep his temper under control (no doubt due to having two highly volatile parents).

Despite that, he couldn't resist the temptation Aisling posed. It was her chin, he told himself later. Her little round, stubborn chin drove his control past all bearing. "Things are already hard, sweetheart," he told her, then gave in to the demands of his body and pulled her to his chest, her body soft and warm and fitting perfectly against him.

As he kissed her, his fire whipped through him with a roar of something akin to hunger, and for a second, his control slipped and it twisted from him to Aisling. Immediately, he started to pull the fire back, not wanting to harm her, but to his immense stupefaction, just as he felt her body heat past the point of bearing, she flipped it back onto him, the shared fire driving his desire to the stratosphere.

He jerked back, but managed to keep his mouth on hers, relishing the sensation of the shared fire, of her body, of the taste of her that filled his mind and pushed his sudden erection to a level of hardness that he couldn't remember experiencing before.

"Maybe you'll think twice about messing with me again," Aisling told him as soon as he managed to pull his mouth from hers.

Christos, the woman tasted like heat and desire and honey. He wanted to kiss her again, and then possess her wholly and completely. Next to him, Pal and István moved a short distance away.

It took Drake a few seconds to focus his mind on things other than his erection, and the need to take Aisling against the nearest private wall. When he had wrestled his libido to a dull roar, he turned to acknowledge the Venediger's arrival.

"Drake, you will do me the honor of introducing me to your companion," Albert said.

He made the introduction, and that was the moment he realized what truly had happened—she'd taken his fire.

No mortal could do so unless she was a mate. But he was a wyvern, and that meant she … he gave a mental headshake. It wasn't right. She couldn't be his mate. She was human.

Every dragon knew that wyverns could not have human mates.

"This is the Guardian you saw earlier?" Pal asked softly in their native Magyar while Aisling continued to argue.

He gave a brief nod, his attention focused on the woman before him.

"She took his fire," István said to Pal.

"She did," Pal agreed. "I don't understand how it is, but she did."

Drake ignored the question of just how Aisling could take his fire when she was mortal, and itched to be rid of the Venediger.

Fortunately, Albert did not dally after meeting Aisling, allowing Drake to give in to his body's demand to be near her. He drew her to his favorite booth, watched as she drank a glass of dragon's blood, and found himself highly amused when she accused him of trying to poison her with it.

It was clear that she was, in fact, exactly what she said—a woman who had just found out she was a Guardian.

What he couldn't wrap his mind around was the inexplicable need that seemed to grow inside his belly, a warmth that went beyond dragon fire. It was as if she had a bond to him that she refused to see, and which he, himself, didn't understand.

Wyverns did not bond themselves to mortals, he reminded himself.

When she left after he refused her awkward attempt to seduce him in order to regain the Anima, Pal and István slid into the booth. Drake watched her return to a table occupied by a Wiccan and her doppelganger, his mind filled with speculation.

"She's mortal," István said in his usual manner of getting straight to the point. "She can't be a wyvern's mate and be mortal."

"I am aware of this fact," Drake said, his eyes still on Aisling. Why did he like that defiant toss of her head when she saw he was watching? Why did he want to march over to her table and demand to know of what she was speaking? What outrageous thoughts did she have that she wasn't sharing with him?

And dammit, why did he care so much? She was just a woman, a single, solitary woman who evidently did not have a very good grasp on her own life, and yet there she was, storming into his, dragging chaos after her.

"I won't have it," he said aloud, narrowing his eyes when he caught one of the mages lounging across the bar ogling Aisling. "She is just a woman, nothing more. I've had hundreds of women over the course of my life. Thousands of them. This one is no different."

István nodded. "Mortals these days are sorely lacking as sexual partners. They're so skittish, and their heads are filled with ideas shoved at them by films and books. It's ridiculous the things they believe about us. Fortunately, I have Suzanne, but I can't imagine how frustrating it is for you to be so spoken to, Drake. That Guardian is out of line in her manner, and will bring you nothing but trouble."

Pal gave Drake a long look that was impossible to interpret. The small smile that accompanied it, however, was all too obviously full of sympathy.

SIX

22 July 2004

She says she is leaving my home. Unbelievable! She said—

"Heya, Drake, Ash told me to tell you that René will be here in ten mins, and she'll be down shortly to say good-bye and all that stuff. Like my backpack? She bought it this morning so I could carry my stuff in it. I think it looks kind of dashing. Also, you shouldn't plan on trying to seduce Aisling into staying, because that crap's not gonna fly."

Jim, the oddly named demon dog, strolled into Drake's library wearing a child's glittery pink backpack strapped around its chest, and interrupted Drake before he could fully put down into his journal his thoughts about Aisling.

He cocked an eyebrow at the demon. "She said that?"

It gave a head bobble. "Well, not the last part. That was me just warning you that she's being all sorts of extra, and my dude, you don't want any part of it."

"As unique an experience as it is to be given advice about my mate from a demon in a fur suit, I believe I will use my own best judgment on the matter," Drake said, his dragon fire riding high. It had been that way since the evening when Aisling refused to acknowledge the truth of their relationship and remained locked in the room he'd given over for her use.

"Whatevs. I'm just warning you that she's in a mood from Abaddon. Can I sit on the couch?"

"No." Drake didn't intend to actually carry out a conversation with the demon, but curiosity got the better of him, and he spent a moment to consider the dog. It sat next to the couch with what Drake thought of as a dopey expression, but he had to allow that the demon's eyes gave proof that it was a lot more astute than he'd first thought. "Why are you remaining with her? You could easily have her assign you to someone else, or break the bond between you together. And yet, you remain."

"Yeah, it's kind of a long story, and it involves a couple of people who probably wouldn't thank me for mentioning them—in fact, I had to swear to one of them that I'd pretend I didn't know her at all—but really, it's a matter of mutual help. Aisling helps me by not letting me be pulled into some other demon lord's service, and I keep all the big, bad dragons from overwhelming her."

Drake only just managed to keep from rolling his eyes. He was an uncomfortable mixture of frustration—sexual and otherwise—and anger that Aisling could so easily throw away her relationship to him and the sept.

"It's unacceptable," he murmured, striding over to the window to glare out of it at nothing in particular. "She is my mate. She should be at my side. It is the way of dragonkin."

"Dunno about all that, but you gotta admit, she pulled off a humdinger of a challenge. I give her a ten out of ten for effectiveness by almost summoning Bael, himself. Not many Guardians out there can do that, you know?"

"I know," Drake said grimly, and for a second had a presentiment of what life would hold for him being mated to a powerful—if untrained—Guardian. The sort who could summon beings well beyond her experience and knowledge. He wondered what the Guardians' Guild would make of her, and, for a moment, thought about whether he could compromise and allow her to get the training she so obviously needed while also remaining at his side, as was right and proper for wyverns' mates. "I did not understand her challenge at first; then I realized she had every intention of losing. It was impossible not to admire the fact that she uncovered the truth of Perdita without any more blood being spilled, but the fact remains that she refuses to accept who and what she is. That I cannot tolerate."

"Don't think you have much of a choice, though, do you?" Jim asked, nosing open an electronics magazine that sat on an ebony coffee table. "Oooh. What's this? Blizzard is starting up a multiplayer game at the end of the year? Man, I used to love playing Warcraft III back when I was at Whiskey Sam's. All of the phone psychics were addicted to it. Hmm. I'll have to check out this new one. Maybe Aisling will buy me a joystick. They're a lot easier to use than a mouse, and not very expensive, right? Yeah. I'll have her get me a joystick."

Drake experienced another one of those painful emotional moments where he acknowledged admiration of Aisling's bravery and ingenuity, but at the same time, the potential power she wielded made him a bit uncomfortable ... and, worse, intrigued to the point of admitting he couldn't live without her.

What he could not see was a life where they lived separately. She would just have to agree with the reason of his thinking and acquiesce to his wisdom.

"Hmm. Wonder if Aisling has a computer back home. She has to, right? I mean, everyone does these days." Jim continued to peruse the magazine, while Drake's thoughts continued to make him uncomfortable.

Wyverns protected their mates. How did Aisling expect him to do so when she was returning to Oregon, and he'd be in Europe?

"What we need is a good desktop computer. One of those jobbies with a lot of RAM and graphics oomph," Jim said, its voice muffled as it turned the page. "Something that can play The Sims, too."

Drake admitted that he was out of his depths when it came to making Aisling see the wisdom of his plans, and immediately pivoted to ways to protect her while he worked on bringing her to his way of thinking.

He looked at the demon dog. "Can you use a mobile phone?"

"Huh? Me? Sure. I use a pencil to punch the buttons. But my phone got left behind at Whiskey Sam's when Aisling summoned me."

"István!" Drake marched to the door, and spoke briefly to Pal, who was passing through the hall. A minute later, Drake tucked a mobile phone into the dog's backpack. "This is a spare phone we keep for emergencies. You will not let Aisling know I gave it to you. Do I make myself clear?"

Jim pursed its lips before giving a brief nod. "You keeping tabs on Aisling through me?"

"That is the idea, yes. If she insists on being stubborn by returning to her home without the intention of joining me as she should, then I must do what I can to protect her. You will report to me any actions which put her in danger." He thought for a moment. "In fact, a daily report would be a good idea. What she does, who she sees, and so on."

"Whoa, whoa, whoa!" The demon backed up a step. "I'm not going to go stalker for you. I'll let you know if that blue dragon Fiat comes sniffing around her again, because he just doesn't smell right, if you know what I mean, but I'm a demon, not a psychopath!"

Drake tamped down the fire that wanted to explode out of him at the idea of Fiat Blu doing something so heinous as trying to take his mate, and instead focused on what was important—Aisling's protection.

He gave the demon another long look. "You have known her for less than a week, and yet you exhibit loyalty and protectiveness. Just what sort of a demon are you?"

"Sixth class all the way, baby," Jim drawled.

"Don't call me baby," Drake said absently, making a swift decision. He knew full well that Aisling would have more than a few things to say if she knew he was going to ensure her safety while he was deliberating on ways to make her understand the true nature between a dragon and his mate. "Very well, I agree to your terms. You will monitor the situation regarding her and will notify me of anything dangerous."

"And in return?" Jim had the nerve to ask.

Drake leaned down so that he could pin the demon back with a look that literally had the carpet beneath the dog's feet smoking. "I don't roast you alive."

"Gotcha," Jim said, backing up until it ran ass-first into the wall. "Sounds good. Thanks for the phone. I don't suppose there's any tracking software or anything on it?"

Drake narrowed his eyes. The tip of the demon's tail lit on fire.

"I was just asking!" Jim said, whirling around a few times to try to catch its tail, which it didn't accomplish, although the movement did put out the flames. "Sheesh! Maybe get some anger management classes while you're waiting."

Drake would have responded, but the demon, seeing the answer in his eyes, bolted through the open door.

"Do you need anything?" Pal asked as he passed the door. "Someone to send the demon back to Abaddon?"

"No." His thoughts felt unusually jumbled, and he struggled to put them in order. "But I recall hearing of an event in a few months in Budapest. I will check to see if my memory is correct."

A half hour later, he sat at his desk in the study that, moments before, had seemed so full of life.

And promise.

And a mate who made his dragon fire leap to impossible heights.

Now, with Aisling having left a few minutes ago, it was just a room, one empty and cold and dimmed despite the sunshine streaming into the window.

He rubbed a spot on his solar plexus, feeling for some reason as if he'd taken a morning star to the gut, and sat down at his desk, pulling out the journal.

22 July 2004

She has left Paris. She handed me the Occhio di Lucifer, and simply walked out. I have arranged—

"Drake, there is an Inspector Proust who wishes to speak with you regarding the imprisonment of the

Wiccan." Pal stood in the doorway to Drake's study and made a wry face. "I put him in the front parlor, since no doubt he would want to speak with Aisling, too."

"She left," Drake said, feeling peevish and more than a little stunned. He'd known she was going to do it, but still, how could she simply walk out on him?

"Ah," Pal said with a nod. "Smart to get out of the way of the mortal police."

"No, she didn't leave to avoid the police." He got to his feet, still feeling as if someone had pulled a very large rug out from under him. "She left me."

"She what?" Pal's expression summed up almost exactly the same sense of disbelief that gripped Drake. "Left for where? István! Did you hear? Aisling has left."

"She has?" István joined Pal and glanced around the study just as if he'd find her lurking in a corner.

Drake embraced the sense of self-righteousness that replaced the disbelief. She was his mate, and she left him. He'd never heard of a mate leaving a wyvern. "She kissed me and then left."

"How can she do that?" Pal asked, rubbing his nose. "She's a mate. A wyvern's mate."

István muttered something about being able to do better, but Drake thought it best to ignore the comment. He was well aware that István harbored suspicions about Aisling, but there was no doubt in Drake's mind that Aisling was, at the very least, sincere. She truly had no clue how to be a Guardian, let alone a wyvern's mate.

"I will have to teach her what it means to be mated to a dragon," he said as he set down the journal and strode toward the hall. "And that she cannot simply wash her hands of me. Of the sept."

"No, she can't. She belongs to us now," Pal agreed.

"And there's the challenge. She failed. She has to pay the penalty," István pointed out, falling into step behind Drake.

"That is of minor concern to me right now," Drake said before throwing open the door to a small, seldom-used parlor, and marching in to meet the detective who had handled the cases of Mme Deauxville and the Venediger.

It took almost an hour to deal with the mortal police, but at last, the final threads were tied up.

"I have frequently found that those who look the guiltiest are often exactly that," Proust said as Drake showed him to the door. He paused on the step and glanced out at the perfectly normal sunny Paris street. "But in the case of Mademoiselle Aisling, I am prepared to concede that she has an uncanny habit of turning up at scenes she would better avoid."

"She has that tendency, yes," Drake agreed, and shut the door firmly on the man, having had about as much aggravation as he could take in one day.

Just as he was returning to his study, his mother called.

"Drakeling!" Catalina's voice was filled with emotion. "You will not believe what your cousin is saying about you in Rio. He says you are not the rightful wyvern. As if I suffered for months to bring you to life, begging the Virgin herself to protect you against the derangement of your father, only for some whelp of a dragon to speak thusly about you. You must avenge such slurs!"

Drake, who was originally headed for the desk, made a detour, snatching up a bottle of dragon's blood before he sank down into a deep leather wingback chair. He didn't even bother with a glass—he swigged it straight from the bottle while his mother continued to rant and rave about something wholly unimportant to him.

"There is a conference happening soon in Budapest," Drake said many hours later. He felt remarkably well despite the situation. The fact that he'd ended up drinking three bottles of dragon's blood might have something to do with that.

"Huh? Who's this? Drake?" Jim the demon's words were slow and half-mumbled.

"Yes, of course it is. I have arranged for registration to be offered to Aisling. Please see to it that she attends the conference."

"Dude. It's like two in the morning and we got into Portland about six hours ago, so we're jet-lagged to Abaddon and back. What conference?"

Drake tried to stand, but it took four tries before he was steady on his feet. "It's called GODTAM. Guardians will be there seeking apprentices. Make sure Aisling understands that she can obtain training from the Guardians who will be present."

István entered, his eyebrows up in an obvious question of whether he should leave.

Drake shook his head, lost his balance, and flopped down on the sofa with less grace than he preferred.

"OK. That's kinda tricky, but you know, I like it. She really does need training. She almost lost her shit a couple of hours ago because some deadbeat surfer dude rolled up and demanded money, saying she was late on alimony. Did you know she had been married to a surfer?"

Rage filled him. Rage, and dragon fire, and a deep need to kiss Aisling until she could think of nothing but him. "Give me every detail you have about this mortal. I will see to it that he no longer bothers Aisling."

"OK, but do you think you could put unlimited data on this phone? 'Cause there's a new Candy Crush out, and I don't have the data for it."

"Give me the information I want, and I will allow you unlimited data," Drake said, hanging up before eyeing a cushion. The sofa was incredibly comfortable. He imagined napping on it would be wonderful.

"Problems?" István asked, moving into the room. He noted the empty bottles but said nothing, just waited for Drake to respond. "The oracle I bribed to get Aisling an invite to the conference says that only the best of the best are invited to it. I hope it's worth all that money to get her there."

It took three minutes before Drake—who'd given in to the temptation offered by the deliciously soft sofa and stretched out on it—managed to rally his thoughts enough to answer. "It will cost more than money if Aisling refuses to see reason."

"Pal thinks she's a powerful Guardian," István said, his expression one of suspicion.

"She is. She is also unlearned."

"So, if she is trained by other Guardians, won't she become that much more powerful?" István asked.

Drake closed his eyes. His body felt empty, as if he was a husk of his former self, the pre-Aisling Drake who had spent his life devoted to the sept. One part of his inebriated mind pointed out that not once since he'd met Aisling had he the desire to bed other women. It was as if that part of his life—the doubts, the fears, the worry over his lack of ability to shift—was erased the second he kissed her in Mme Deauxville's apartment.

Now there was only Aisling.

"Drake?" István picked up the bottles, clearly allowing them to clink loudly.

"I will make sure things don't go that far," he answered, then closed his eyes and allowed the alcohol to numb him to the emptiness inside.

SEVEN

24 July 2004

The dreams have started again.

Drake tapped the pen on the journal, wondering whether he should make a notation of the phenomenon that he hadn't experienced since he was a youngling dragon.

It had to have meaning. He would note it.

The dream began as they all did, with a half awareness that something was beyond normal.

"Grand-mère?" The words lifted on the breeze that rolled inland from the shore.

Drake glanced around and realized he was standing in the small garden of his grandmother's villa outside Cannes.

She turned, holding a bouquet of her favorite flowers—pink and white carnations—surprise chased by delight as she beheld him. "Drake! What brings you to see me? Is all well?"

He received two featherlight kisses on his cheeks, her familiar spicy flower scent surrounding him with love. He basked in it for a moment before responding,

"Nothing is awry, although I am not sure why I am here. I have not visited you in a dream since …"

"Since you went through puberty, yes," Grand-mère said as she nodded, then moved past him, glancing with pleasure around her garden. "We had many visits during your youth, did we not? Ah, I remember that wall with the columbines! How pretty they were. This was always my favorite villa. Did you keep it after I died?"

"Yes," Drake said, wondering if the recent highly erotic dream experience with Aisling had meant a return of his long dormant ability. "Why am I having dreams visiting you now? It was understandable when you were alive, but …"

"But that is no longer the case. Something must have happened," Grand-mère said before murmuring words of delight as she continued to stroll around the garden. "Such lovely pinks. I've always felt roses were a bit ostentatious, but really, these tea roses were not at all of that class. I must see about changing our domicile to one of a house with a garden. What has changed in your life, *kincsem*?"

Silence followed the question. Drake frowned as he wondered how to explain the experience of the last week. "I met a Guardian," he answered at last. "She had an artifact I desired."

"And you relieved her of the item?" Piroska tipped her head to the side, a smile curling the corners of her mouth. "Why do I even ask? Always you were extremely adept at acquiring items you desired."

"Yes, I took it," he said absently, trying to sort through his emotions. "She—the Guardian—is a wyvern's mate."

"Drake!" Grand-mère clapped her hands with joy before kissing his cheeks again. "I am so happy for you.

And you did not think you would ever find a mate. That's why you must have dreamt of me again—you knew I would not rest easy in the afterlife until I knew you had found a mate."

"She won't have anything to do with me," he admitted, sitting on the wrought iron bench when Grand-mère gestured to it, taking her own seat.

Bees buzzed happily behind them, while before them both, the garden sloped down to a sparkling white beach, beyond which the sea glistened and glittered a brilliant cerulean.

The contrast between the idyllic scene and the hellish nightmare of his emotions did not escape him. "She refuses to accept she is a mate." The words seemed to come out slowly, as if he was encased in ice. "She left me. I put the sept mark on her, and she still left."

Grand-mère seemed to hear the mingled frustration and hurt that laced his words, for she took one of his hands in hers and gave it a gentle squeeze. "It is like that, is it? I do not fear you will do as your father and force her to accept you, for you are not in the least bit like Toldi, but still, a mate is not to be dismissed. What are you doing to woo her?"

"Nothing," Drake answered, the word leaving a bitter taste in his mouth. "She has returned to her home and refuses to remain in contact with me."

"Ah," Grand-mère said, and, releasing his hand, rose, clearly going to head back into the villa. "That is why you are dreaming again. It has been pleasant seeing you again, but, my Drake, it is not to the past you must look, but to your future."

Before he could answer, the dream wafted away into nothing, just as if it were fog evaporating before the potent rays of the sun.

He opened his eyes, staring up at the familiar ceiling of his bedroom, and wondered just what the hell Grand-mère meant by that.

25 July 2004
Grand-mère was correct.

Drake stepped out of the shadow of a smallish one-story house, glancing around to pinpoint just where his dream had taken him. He was once again on the shoreline, this time right on the beach, the scrubby, stunted grass underfoot mixed with sand and dotted with scraggly shrubs.

The door of the cabin opened and Aisling stood there, her hair whipping around with the breeze off the water, while her eyes came damned close to shooting lasers at him.

"No!" she said, then slammed shut the door.

Drake fought the need to simply storm into the house and demand she recognize the fact that she was his mate, aware that would be all too close to the actions of his father.

"I've never before understood why he did what he did, but I'm starting to see it now," he muttered to himself, the dream fading until he found himself once again lying in bed, staring up at the lights of the city as they skittered across the ceiling.

The following night, he settled into bed and schooled his mind into a rehearsal of what he would say to Aisling, how she would respond, and how graciously he'd welcome her home as his mate.

The dream was the same as the night before. It was late night on a beach, the moon's light skipping across the crest of the waves as they reached inky fingers onto golden brown sand.

He tapped at the door.

"I said no!" Aisling all but snarled when she opened the door, once again glaring at him. This time he had the presence of mind to stick his foot into the doorway, keeping her from slamming the door on him.

She gave it a good try, though.

"Peste!" he swore, jerking back and hopping on the uninjured foot as he felt his toes to see if they'd been broken when she tried to force the door closed.

"Yes, you are. Go away, Drake. I said we were done, and we're done."

The door was closed again in his face, just as forcefully as it had been the previous night.

He retreated from the dream, sitting in bed as he absently rubbed his bruised toes, his mind quickly sorting through a number of options and discarding anything that smacked too much of Toldi.

"I want Aisling in my life," he told his abused toes. "But I want her to want to be here."

The following three visits to Aisling's cabin at the sea ended the same as the first two, minus the sore toes.

But it was the sixth dream where he stopped thinking like a wyvern, and decided to tackle Aisling a different way.

"What's this?" she asked suspiciously when she opened the door and discovered the square box with green ribbon he'd placed on her doorstep. "The aquamanile?"

He simply cocked an eyebrow at her.

"I didn't think so." Her face bore a decidedly disgruntled expression. She nudged the box with her foot. "What is it?"

"Open it," he told her, leaning against the side of her cabin, his arms crossed.

"OK, but if it's something that hurts me—" She stopped before he had the chance to be outraged at the idea of such a thing. She lifted her hand. "No, you don't have to say it. I'm sorry for implying I believe you'd harm me. But, Drake, we have to stop meeting like this! For one, I left you last week. I … left … you. And for another, I'm hardly getting any sleep what with you popping into my dreams every night, and Jim's comments about the bags under my eyes are getting over the top to the point where I'm seriously thinking about ordering it into the form of a cement block. A silent one. So please … oooh."

While she had been speaking, he removed the ribbon from the box, and lifted the lid. Inside it sat a Sacher torte made by his favorite chef.

"Is that … a cake?" Aisling asked, peering into the box when he lifted it for her inspection.

"Yes. You like cake." He offered the box to her.

"Oooh. Is it that Austrian one you had when I was staying with you?" She dipped her finger into a mound of chocolate and whipped cream that adorned the cake, then licked it off in a manner that left Drake immediately hard. "Mmm. It is. OK, this cake has bought you five minutes to talk, assuming that's what you are here for, but only because that's how long it will take me to finish off the whole thing. And don't look at me like I'm being selfish by not even offering you any. It's a dream, and you're crazy if you think I'm not going to take advantage of the fact that I can eat this entire thing without any result on my hips."

To Drake's amusement, she dug her fingers into the torte with a glint in her eyes that reminded him of his mother when she was at her most outrageous. He didn't at all comment on how messy it was to eat cake with her bare hands, and instead gave voice to what was uppermost on his mind.

"You miss me," he found himself saying. For a moment, he gave a mental eye roll at the words. He was an erudite man, one who prided himself on the manners his grand-mère found attractive, and to blurt something so baldly was unlike him.

"Yeah," she answered around a mouthful of cake, popping a chocolate-and-whipped-cream finger into her mouth to suck off all the goodness.

He grew even harder, and for a good minute, all he could think of was how she filled his senses, how she tasted, what her silky, delicious skin felt like against his, and most of all, how right she was. He'd never truly believed in the validity of mates, given his family history, but Aisling … Aisling was different. She enraged him, true, but she also fit so well—both physically and on a dragon level—that he was beginning to understand the emptiness that echoed inside him had its beginning and end with the curly-haired woman who stood before him stuffing her face with an entire Sacher torte.

Warmth flooded all the dark corners of his soul at the sight.

"That doesn't mean anything, though. I'm trying to cut out refined carbs, and I miss them a hell of a lot, too," she continued while he was wrestling with the need to bury himself in her, and revel in the sharing of his dragon fire. "But that doesn't mean I'm going to let them back into my life, where they can control me and take advantage of me, and just in general annoy me with their irresistibleness. I am a professional, Drake. I can handle having no sugar just like I can handle having no sexy green-eyed dragon stomping around in my life."

He looked pointedly at her right hand, which was holding a piece of cake.

"This doesn't count," she snapped, defiantly biting at the remainder. "It's dream cake. It has no calories. I just said that. Didn't you listen?"

"I heard you," he said, trying to retain his sense of calm, but she made it very difficult to not give in to his inner dragon.

At last he understood why his father had done what he'd done. Not that Drake condoned the killing of innocent mortals, but he understood the extremes that Toldi had gone to in order to bind Catalina to him.

"Why are you here?" she asked, murmuring her thanks when she took the handkerchief and moistened towelette he offered before wiping her sticky hands with it. "What's so important you had to barge into my brain with an absolutely delicious dream cake that won't add a single ounce to my hips and thighs?"

It was on the tip of his tongue to tell her he liked her hips and thighs, liked them far too much for his own peace of mind, but instead he sat down on the sandy wooden porch, deciding that his plan to share a secret from his past would show her that he trusted her. He could think of no way to prove his dedication to her.

The Pacific Ocean lay before them, an undulating mass of sound and scent. Drake stared into it, plucking through the mists of time to uncover the ulcer of shame that even now gave him a moment of remembered pain.

"Drake?" Aisling yawned. "Dragon got your tongue?"

He turned to her, confused. "What dragon?"

"It was supposed to be a funny variation of 'cat got your tongue,' but I can see it went right over your head."

She yawned again. "It's because I'm super sleepy and not making sense, and now my dream self has eaten like a week's worth of carbs, so I'm about to go back to sleep. What was it you wanted to tell me?"

"When I was a young dragon, probably about twenty or so years, I spent my days with three other green dragons," he said slowly, hoping to find a way to explain the guilt that still ate at him at unexpected moments. "This was in Buda."

"Budapest? Hungary?" Aisling asked.

He was very aware of her sitting next to him, aware of the heat of her body, and the scent that teased his nose despite the tangy air rolling in with the gentle surf. "This was in the seventeenth century, so the part I lived in was simply called Buda. My 'company of troublemakers,' as my grandmother referred to us, acted no different than any other young men at the time—we trained in arms, we drank far too much bad wine and ale, we dallied with the mortal women—" He moved on quickly when Aisling jerked to the side, his subsequent words coming out in an undignified tumble. "We fought, we jousted, we hunted … it was our lives."

"A group of dragon toughs, in other words," Aisling said softly, but he felt her interest. He was also aware when she stopped recoiling from him and actually brushed his arm with hers.

"Not in the modern sense, no, but something similar. There was no malice in us, just high spirits." He paused, the old pain stinging. "Until that night. We were drunk, and stumbled out into the streets, my friends accosting mortal women."

"For the love of Saint Pete!" Aisling said, this time not recoiling, but she actually separated herself from him, standing at the base of the three steps to glare at him. "You sexually assaulted someone? Do you know how heinous—"

"Pax," he said, holding up his hand. He wanted badly to be righteously indignant that his mate, his own mate, would think he could do anything so vile, but the common sense that came from his grandparents reminded him she did not know him well.

Yet.

"I did not then, nor have I ever forced myself on a woman," he told her, allowing her to feel the fire that swirled inside him at the slander.

"I should hope not," Aisling said, and, after a couple of seconds' obvious struggle, retook her seat next to him. "So if you weren't pillaging and raping, what is it your gang of thugs did?"

"What you would call roughhousing, I suppose," he said after a moment's thought. "Stealing a bit of fruit or bread. Stirring up the merchants. Teasing a few of the more pompous mortals. It was relatively harmless until I decided to assert my dominance over my friends. I was in the running to be named heir, and looking back with the wisdom of time, I see that it had gone to my head. I was determined to prove to them that I was the natural leader, so instead of just picking up a mortal's basket of goods and teasing her with it before returning it, I knocked a woman's small basket of food to the ground, and stomped on it."

Aisling gave him a long look out of the corners of her eyes. "OK, that seems pretty out of character for you."

"Whether it was or not doesn't change the outcome. My friends laughed and mocked the woman as she fell to her knees and tried to salvage whatever bit of bread and potage had survived my boots. As my friends continued to the next tavern, the woman hunched over her destroyed food, weeping."

Aisling said nothing, but blinked rapidly, clearly waiting for him to continue.

The shame burned in him with an intensity that came close to matching his dragon fire. "She looked up and, through her tears, asked me why I did it. 'Does it make you feel like a big man to take food out of my hungry children's mouths? Are you proud of making my family go without food simply because you have strength we don't? There is death everywhere, and you must hasten its path by starving my children?' Her words pierced me with the full shame of my actions, leaving me filled with mortification and dismay."

"That last was a bit flowery, but I understand how horrible the situation was." Aisling gave him another long look. "For the woman, that is; you don't get to play victim, although I assume you gave her money."

"I just told you how I shamelessly and carelessly destroyed a woman's only food, and you assume I gave her money?" he asked, his head tipping to the side as he considered her face.

It was a nice face. He liked it. He especially liked that her emotions were plainly visible to him, laid out like a delightful book to read.

"I may not know you well, Drake, but I do know you're not a cruel man. Not toward non-dragons, that is," she answered.

"If I am, it is because my grand-mère devoted herself to the well-being of mortals around her, and tried hard to get me to do the same," he answered, uncomfortable with the praise she had inadvertently given him. "As it happens, I did give the woman the coins I had with me. I left her still weeping over her spilled dinner, but at least she held the few coins I had. The shame of my actions haunted me, however. I could not bear to admit to my grandmother—with whom I was living—what I'd done. The following morning, I loaded a wagon with goods and tried to find the mortal woman, but she had disappeared. A plague was in Buda then, so it's likely she succumbed to that. I do not know. I never found her."

"Ouch," Aisling said, nodding slowly. "You never got your moment of redemption. I take it this still rankles even though it's been literally hundreds of years?"

"What rankles, as you put it, is the fact that I was never able to make reparation to the woman for my thoughtless actions. In the scheme of things, the life of one woman and her children do not matter overmuch, but …" He braced for shame to lash him with its barbed hooks, but to his surprise, it had lessened a bit.

"But you are not so callous as to buy into that sort of misanthropic attitude," Aisling finished for him.

He inclined his head. "It is a shame I bear nonetheless. Through my own arrogance I harmed a mortal woman, a being weaker than me, one my grandmother would say demanded my protection because of that weakness. And I treated her with contempt and ridicule."

"You know, if you were any other person, I'd say you were fishing for a compliment. Or at least, if not a compliment, then reassurance that what you did was not so bad, and you made up for it." Aisling put her hand on his leg and gave him a quick pat. "But I suspect instead you've internalized everything, and are letting it fester."

"Fester is a good description," he agreed. "Although I don't seek redemption in your eyes, if that's what you're thinking. I want you to understand me better, even though it is painful to bare my shame with you."

She shook her head, rising even as she spoke. "I appreciate that, I really do. And if I had a soul-searing admission to make, other than the stupidity of me being eighteen and marrying the first beach bum who flexed at me, I'd reciprocate, but it doesn't mean I'm going to run into your open arms. I think our wires are crossed, Drake. You believe I'm meant to be your trusty sidekick, and I think I'm a main character who has a whole new world to explore and learn about. And I'm going to do that."

"Are the two things mutually exclusive?" he asked, slowly getting to his feet, as well. Oddly, he felt lighter, as if his admission had healed some of the pain that remained for four hundred years.

She hesitated at the open doorway before disappearing into it. "You tell me."

He had no answer to that. Not one he wanted to give her.

The dream slipped away, leaving him feeling bereft once more.

EIGHT

31 July 2004

He stood glaring out a rain-splattered window, staring at a grayish-blue turbulent Pacific Ocean.

"We could have taken care of this without having to fly all the way from France to Oregon," István pointed out as he, too, examined the scene before them with a jaded look. "The kin in California would have dealt with the mortal."

"It is not their problem," Drake said with a calmness that belied his true emotions. He was annoyed. He was enraged. And most of all, he was frustrated.

Why could Aisling not see that she was meant to bind herself to him? That they were fated to be together?

"No, but they would be happy to help," István insisted, then flexed his knuckles.

Drake glanced at his watch, his temper—and emotions—firmly in check. Even his dragon fire was under steely control to the point where it barely simmered inside him.

Just the thought of Aisling licking whipped cream off her fingers had it roaring to life, though.

"It is almost time," Drake said, and closed the laptop he'd been using while they waited for Aisling's mortal ex-husband to appear for the day. Their hotel overlooked one of the parking areas on Cannon Beach.

"You want me to go out to see if he's there?" István asked, curling his lip at the rain. While it was true that green dragons favored water, the element tied to the sept, very few enjoyed being out in the rain.

"Yes, but you needn't stalk up and down the beach. Remain in the car and let me know when he arrives."

István looked doubtful. "Is it likely the rain will stop?"

"Surfers, I am given to understand, will surf in the summer even if it's raining." Drake's phone rang as István headed out to the rental car.

"Is something the matter?" he asked in lieu of greeting the caller.

A few seconds of various muffled and somewhat thumping noises were audible, along with the rhythmic noise of breathing, and unintelligible words by a man. This was followed by a louder thump, at which point the voices could be understood.

"—don't see why you're holding it against me. The police cleared me!"

Aisling was speaking. Drake, who had been on the verge of demanding to know why Jim had called him, stood holding the phone, his eyes narrowed on it. Clearly Jim had put the phone on speaker and moved it into position to overhear the conversation.

Drake made a mental note to send the demon virtual funds for its phone game.

"Evidently, they even sent me a reward, which of course I'll give to you to go a little ways to make up for the aquamanile being sold. I know it won't cover the part the insurance refused to reimburse you for, but it will help, and as I said a week ago, I'll do whatever jobs you need to pay off the rest."

"It's not the money," a man's gruff voice answered her. Drake felt a particularly itchy sensation that he equated with hackles rising. "It's you. You're not right for the job. You gave it your best shot, but it's not going to cut it, Aisling."

"I can do better," she said, and for a moment rage rode him hard. Who was this man who so berated his mate? How dare he blame her for what had happened in Paris? Drake had made very certain that Proust, the mortal police inspector, had cleared Aisling of all wrongdoing. "Just give me a chance, Uncle Damian."

"I gave you a chance. You let the object be stolen from you, and the recipient was murdered. Along with a whole slew of other folks, it seems, but I won't get into that, since I didn't sell them the object."

"I'm innocent of that! Of everything except inadvertently burning ... but that's not really important. Here's the check the French police gave me for helping them figure out who the murderer of Madame Deaux-ville was."

Drake snarled under his breath. That money was meant to entice Aisling into going to Budapest!

"Please, Uncle Damian, please give me a second chance. I swear I won't let another item be stolen from me. Although it would ... er ... really help if the object wasn't made of gold. Just in case. Do you have anything nongold that has to go somewhere?"

"Yes, but I'll get one of the other couriers to take it."

"But—"

"No," Aisling's uncle cut across her protest. "That's the end of it."

"You are the most stubborn, annoying person I've met." Aisling stopped herself in mid-rant to say, "OK, that's not entirely true. The most stubborn, annoying person I've met is in Paris right now, but you're right there beside him!"

"Give my respects to David and Paula when you next talk to them," was all her uncle said.

"Gah!" Loud footsteps sounded along with a, "Jim, heel!"

Drake could almost imagine the scene as Aisling stalked out the door. He added to his list of things to question Aisling the identity of this David and Paula her uncle mentioned. He assumed they were family, but it drove home the point that he had no idea about who—other than her uncle and an ex-husband—were important people in her life.

Dealing with the beach bum ex turned out to be quick and easy.

"You will cease harassing Aisling for money," Drake told the man, whose face was red and somewhat bloated.

He squawked something in response.

"I don't care what the court order decrees," Drake responded, guessing what the man was protesting. "She will no longer pay you so much as another cent."

The man, one Colm Murphy by name, gurgled and twitched.

Drake's fingers convulsed where they held the man up by the throat. With a little shake, he released Colm, unmoved by the gasping and garbled words that emerged as the ex-husband slid down the stone back wall of an outdoor beach shower.

"I will, however, ensure that the same sum is deposited into your account for exactly six months. After that, you will be responsible for supporting yourself. If you try to contact Aisling again, I will destroy you. If you try to harass her again, I will destroy you. If you try to get money from her, I will—"

"Destroy me, I know," Colm said, trying to get to his feet and failing, one hand still massaging his neck. His voice sounded as rough as the massive Haystack Rock that towered over the beach. "Like, I get it. You're hooking up and all. But that doesn't mean you have to choke me."

"I'll do a hell of a lot worse than choke you if you bother Aisling again," was all he said before striding off to the car, István silent behind him.

"That's one," he said a few minutes later when he got into the car, István at the wheel. He checked his phone, read a message from Pal, who'd remained in Paris to deal with some business there, answered it, and then gave István the address he'd looked up shortly after Jim's call.

"Who's two?" István asked.

Drake consulted his phone again. "Damian Bell."

István's brows rose, but he said nothing.

It took an hour to find the building Aisling's uncle used to run his acquisition and export business, and within five minutes of arriving, he beheld a shortish, thickset man with a rectangular face, a gray beard and hair, and piercing blue eyes.

Drake frowned at him for a few seconds. "Are you related to Ernest Hemingway?" he asked after greeting the man.

Damian Bell's expression was set in a mixture of disfavor and distrust. "No, and I don't know why the devil people keep asking me that. Are you one of those literary people?"

"Not to my knowledge," Drake answered, and since he judged that polite manners would be wasted on the forthright and gruff man before him, he discarded the lengthy explanations he'd formed on the ride there, and got straight to the point. "I met your niece in Paris."

"Aisling?" Bell's eyes narrowed to blue slits. "You the one she shacked up with, or the thief?"

"Both," Drake answered, taking immense pleasure in the moment of shock that filled the man's eyes. "I am Drake Vireo."

"Why are you here?" Bell asked, moving up in Drake's estimation. Although he was well versed in the mostly European method of dancing around a subject with polite chat, he much preferred people who spoke as they thought.

It was one reason Aisling intrigued him so much. He never knew what she'd say.

"To give you this." Drake pulled out a certified check and set it on the desk. "It is payment for the aquamanile, which now resides in my collection. With this, you will consider Aisling's debt paid in full, and will return to her the reward money from the French police."

"Why do you want her to have the money?" Damian Bell glanced at the check, his expression as unwavering as stone. "You can't have designs on it if you're handing me a check this size."

"I believe Aisling has great potential," Drake said after a moment's thought to pick out his words. He had to tread carefully here, lest Aisling's uncle become obstinate. "She has recently explored some new … hobbies … and there is a conference in Budapest which would help her explore them further."

Bell watched him with a silence that made the fine hairs on the back of Drake's neck rise. He had done a quick dig into the man's past in order to garner information about him, but he hadn't had time to delve into much. He recalled there was a mention of service in a branch of the armed forces, and was instantly certain that Bell's time in the military included some sort of black ops work.

"Do you agree?" Drake was forced to ask when Bell continued to simply watch him.

"To giving back the check? I don't have it. I put it in her pocket when she was marching around waving her hands in the air and yelling. As to the other—I don't know what this hobby is that you think she needs help with, but Aisling is an adult. She makes her own choices. I stay out of it unless it affects me or she asks for help." His gaze was sharp as he stared Drake down. "You don't affect me now that you've paid for the aquamanile, and Aisling hasn't asked me to help deal with you."

Drake dipped his head in acknowledgment. "Then we are in agreement."

"Just know," Damian Bell called after him as he turned to leave, his hand on the doorknob. "If you do anything to hurt her—physically or emotionally—you won't regret it."

Drake paused at the door, confused. "I won't?"

"You won't be alive to regret anything," was the response.

He thought for a moment, then nodded his head and said, "I agree to your terms," before leaving the office.

7 August 2004

For a week, Drake felt like an automaton going about his business devoid of emotion, feeling, and hope.

He settled in his house in the countryside outside Budapest, restless and unhappy.

Then he received a text message.

JIM

Heya. Aisling's storming around swearing that you're trying to bribe your way into her pants, and other outrageous things like that. I mean, I get it, but yeah, this was kind of a low blow just up and sending her money. Gotta say one thing about Aisling: she's got a hell of a moral compass. She tried to give the money to her uncle, but he slipped it back to her. She's blaming you for that. She says you engineered the whole thing, and that it's blood money, yadda yadda.

ME

I did not send the money. I believe it came from the French government as a reward for the arrest and conviction of the murderer of the mortal Mme Deauxville and Albert Camus. In such cases, there should be a letter accompanying the check indicating the source and reason for the payment.

JIM

Yeah, yeah, but Ash swears it's a forgery. I'll tell her to check with the French police. That should calm her ta-tas.

JIM

It's just kinda odd that the money the French sent her is the exact amount needed for airfare, hotel, and the conference that's coming up in Budapest.

JIM

Someone told me that the green dragons are based more or less in Hungary. Kinda coinkydink, that, huh?

ME

I regret ever giving you this phone.

See to it she reads the paperwork accompanying the check.

Alert me if she is in any danger.

JIM

Man, you got it bad. Just hope some day Aisling realizes that.

ME

From your mouth to any deity of your choice's ears.

Two nights later, he entered the dream state again that allowed him to visit Aisling.

He stood on the beach and eyed her cottage, wondering if she missed him. Did she dream of him? Did she think about him during the day as he thought of her? Did she remember the way she turned to molten fire under his touch?

He ignored the erection that followed such musings, and tapped at the door.

"Don't tell me, it's a big, bad dragon come to blow my house down." Aisling opened the door. She was clad in a pair of striped cotton shorts and a tank top, neither of which hid any part of her delicious curves.

"Would it shock you if I made a comment about blowing in reference to yourself?" he asked, leaning nonchalantly against the doorframe. It wasn't easy to pull off that expression given the erection, but he gave it his best shot.

"Yes," she answered, then, with an odd look at him, moved past to where two white wooden chairs sat. She stood in front of one of the chairs, staring out at the ocean for a few seconds. "You're a lot of things, Drake, but a crass person is not one of them. That still leaves me wondering why you are here, though."

"We parted in a less-than-ideal manner," he said, ignoring her scent, which wafted to him on the breeze. He needed to keep his attention focused. "You seem to think that a relationship between us is optional. It is not the way, Aisling. We are fated to be together. For you to ignore what is between us is the sheerest folly."

"What's between us?" she asked, taking him by surprise.

He knew what she was asking, however, and gave her the honest answer she was due, even if he felt oddly awkward speaking the words. "I do not know the shape our lives together will take, but if you seek reassurances that you are necessary to me, then you may have them. I want you, Aisling. In my bed, in my sept, in my life. As a wyvern, I will swear an oath to keep your happiness uppermost always."

She was silent for a few minutes, her gaze never leaving his. To his horror, her eyes grew shiny with tears. She blinked fast twice before finally speaking. "If you knew how hard it was for me to leave you, to walk out the door in Paris when you were looking so gorgeous, and mysterious, and the way you smelled and felt ... if you knew the pain that grips me each time I see you—even if it is only in a dream—you wouldn't say that."

"You weep?" He brushed at a fat tear that rolled down one cheek, for a moment at a loss as to what he could do.

"Yes. I do. Because of you. Please, Drake. I'm trying to get a grip on a whole lot of changes in my life, and you're not making it any easier. Quite the opposite, in fact."

He stepped back, feeling physical pain at her rejection. "I do not mean harm to you—"

"No, you don't. I know that." Aisling wrapped her arms around herself, half turning away from him. "But it's almost impossible to get my life in control when you keep popping in and making me feel all sorts of things that I don't want to feel."

"We are mated—"

"No, Drake. We aren't." She turned to face him, tears still glinting brightly in her eyes. "I don't know how else to say this, but I don't want to see you again. I can't be what you want, OK? I've decided I'm going to pursue being a Guardian. There's a big shindig in Europe in a few weeks, and they offered me a spot since they are nurturing new Guardians, and as the money you made the French police send me will cover it, Jim and I are going. I can't be what you want. So if you don't mind, please buzz off and leave me alone."

Pain was evident in her voice. For a moment, he felt the same sort of shame he'd experienced with the starving woman.

His presence in her dreams was hurting her. It was the last thing in the world he wanted, and he realized that he was going to have to practice an exquisite amount of patience if he was going to survive wooing her to his side.

And that meant he had to give her the space she clearly wanted.

"Naturally, the last thing I desire is to make you unhappy," he said after several seconds of fighting with himself. "Since it is your wish to live life without me, I will remove myself from your presence. Know this, though." He was unable to stop from stroking his thumb across her cheek. It almost killed him, but he kept from claiming her mouth as his mind, body, and most primal dragon soul demanded. "If you ever need me, no matter what the circumstances, no matter what the reason, I will be at your side."

She sniffled, brushed angrily at her tears, and nodded before rising and swiftly returning to her house.

It took him longer to leave. He hung around the outside for a few minutes, just watching the ocean under the light of the moon, then finally turned and walked out of the dream.

Aisling may not wish to admit it, but every fiber of Drake's being recognized her as his mate. He would wait for her to come to him. There was nothing else to do.

CALL ME, MAYBE?

My lovely one! I hope you enjoyed reading DRAG-ON REVISITED and BECOMING EFFRIJIM, both of which I handcrafted from the finest artisanal words just for you. If you are new to my dragon books, and want to see more about Drake, Aisling, Jim, and all the other denizens of the Otherworld, feel free to dive into YOU SLAY ME, the first book in the Aisling Grey, Guardian series.

Want more? Join my newsletter at katiemacalister. com for news, exclusive reader bonuses like sneak peaks, extra scenes, and bonus epilogues. It's free and fun. And full of weirdness. Admittedly, lots of weirdness…

ABOUT KATIE

Bird skeleton washer.

Doll's house salesperson to royalty.

King Tut tour guide.

Katie MacAlister has not just worked odd jobs, she's lived an even odder life. Luckily, she's always had a book with her to take her away from the weirdness.

Two years after she started writing novels, Katie sold her first romance, Noble Intentions. More than seventy books later, her novels have been translated into numerous languages, been recorded as audiobooks, received several awards, and have been regulars on the *New York Times*, *USA Today*, *Wall Street Journal*, and *Publishers Weekly* bestseller lists. Katie is a widow who lives in the Pacific Northwest with two dogs, and can often be found lurking around online.

You are welcome to join Katie's official discussion group on Facebook, as well as connect on Instagram. For more information, visit: katiemacalister.com

Made in the USA
Las Vegas, NV
04 October 2023

78541938R00088